# Trick Shot

Cooper snarled, "Move, Adams, or I'll put a bullet in the sheriff."

"Would he do that, McKay?" Clint asked.

"Yeah," McKay said, "he's just stupid enough to do it."

"Well, then, you better drop."

"Wha—" Cooper asked, but suddenly McKay went limp and hit the ground.

Clint hated trick shots. When he _____ hot to kill, but he had never killed a lawman in ____ ___st, not one that hadn't turned. Cooper ___ ____ ___ ugh, so Clint drew and fired whil_ ___ ___ ed. The bullet hit him in the rig___ ___ ___ from his hand to the ground ___ ___ stood up, and backed away.

Cooper wen_ ___ ___ ck plain on his face.

"You didn't kil_ ___ d.

Clint nodded, "I w__ ___ g to . . ."

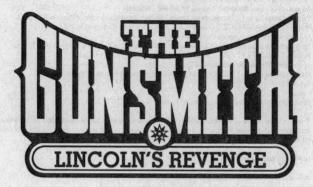

# LINCOLN'S REVENGE

## J. R. ROBERTS

JOVE BOOKS, NEW YORK

**THE BERKLEY PUBLISHING GROUP**
**Published by the Penguin Group**
**Penguin Group (USA) Inc.**
**375 Hudson Street, New York, New York 10014, USA**
Penguin Group (Canada), 90 Eglinton Avenue East, Suite 700, Toronto, Ontario M4P 2Y3, Canada
(a division of Pearson Penguin Canada Inc.)
Penguin Books Ltd., 80 Strand, London WC2R 0RL, England
Penguin Group Ireland, 25 St. Stephen's Green, Dublin 2, Ireland (a division of Penguin Books Ltd.)
Penguin Group (Australia), 250 Camberwell Road, Camberwell, Victoria 3124, Australia
(a division of Pearson Australia Group Pty. Ltd.)
Penguin Books India Pvt. Ltd., 11 Community Centre, Panchsheel Park, New Delhi—110 017, India
Penguin Group (NZ), 67 Apollo Drive, Rosedale, North Shore 0632, New Zealand
(a division of Pearson New Zealand Ltd.)
Penguin Books (South Africa) (Pty.) Ltd., 24 Sturdee Avenue, Rosebank, Johannesburg 2196,
South Africa

Penguin Books Ltd., Registered Offices: 80 Strand, London WC2R 0RL, England

This is a work of fiction. Names, characters, places, and incidents either are the product of the author's imagination or are used fictitiously, and any resemblance to actual persons, living or dead, business establishments, events, or locales is entirely coincidental.

LINCOLN'S REVENGE

A Jove Book / published by arrangement with the author

PRINTING HISTORY
Jove edition / November 2009

Copyright © 2009 by Robert J. Randisi.
Cover illustration by Sergio Giovine.

ISBN: 978-0-515-14730-8

JOVE®
Jove Books are published by The Berkley Publishing Group,
a division of Penguin Group (USA) Inc.,
375 Hudson Street, New York, New York 10014.
JOVE® is a registered trademark of Penguin Group (USA) Inc.
The "J" design is a trademark of Penguin Group (USA) Inc.

PRINTED IN THE UNITED STATES OF AMERICA

10  9  8  7  6  5  4  3  2  1

# ONE

They thought he was crazy, but he was crazy like a fox. Escaping from the asylum was not very hard. After all, it wasn't a prison. He had learned many things over the years, and picking locks was just one of them. There were three locks between him and freedom. He waited till after dark, then picked them one by one and got out.

He wasn't missed until morning.

"How did this happen?" the sheriff of Topeka, Kansas, demanded.

"Look," the director said, "we're a hospital, not a prison."

"No, you're an asylum, filled with crazy people," the sheriff said. "You should have guards on every door."

"We don't have guards, we have attendants," the man said, "and doctors and nurses."

"Then you should have attendants on every door," the sheriff said.

"Look, this man is not dangerous—"

"He fired a weapon at the complete assemblage of the Kansas House of Representatives!"

"He fired over their heads."

"He was only supposed to be a doorman," the sheriff said. "Instead he breaks in on the meetin' and starts shootin' up the place."

"Well, if you thought he was a criminal, you should have put him in prison," the director said. "As I told you, this is a hospital."

The sheriff heaved a sigh. He was going to get nowhere with this man.

"All right," he said. "I'll have to go back to town and get up a posse."

The lawman headed for the door.

"And when you catch him," the director said, standing up, "don't bring him back here. Put him in jail!"

The sheriff ignored the man, marched out of the building, mounted his horse, and rode back to Topeka. He just hoped the escapee was still on foot.

In Topeka the sheriff found his deputy in the office and told him they were going to have to gather a posse.

"What for?"

"Escaped prison— Well, escaped patient from the asylum."

"One of them lunatics got out?"

"Yeah, and we're gonna have to bring him back."

"Which one?" the deputy asked.

"That Lincoln one."

The deputy's eyes went wide.

"The one who calls himself 'Lincoln's Avenger'?" he asked. "He's real interestin'."

"Maybe he is," the sheriff said, "but whatever he is, we got to bring him back. And when we do, they don't want 'im."

"So what are we gonna do with him?"

"That ain't for us to decide," the sheriff said. "We'll leave that to the court."

"The judge?" the deputy asked, laughing. "He's a Lincoln nut. He'll never send the Avenger to jail."

"Look, that ain't up to us," the sheriff said. "Just get out there and find us some bodies."

The deputy stood up, grabbed his hat.

"Any bodies?"

"No," the sheriff said, sitting behind the desk, "bodies that have a brain attached."

"That ain't gonna be easy," the deputy said.

"Tell me about it," the lawman said. "Now go, do the best you can. I want to get movin' as soon as possible."

"Today?"

"No," the sheriff said, "it's already late afternoon. First thing in the mornin'."

"Is he on foot, or horseback?"

"He started out on foot," the sheriff said. "After that, who knows?"

"Okay," the deputy said, "I know of a few men I can ask, but I don't know what they'll say. It ain't like the bank was robbed and they got an interest in bringing the guy back, you know?"

"Well," the sheriff said, "if we have to, you and me'll go."

"And who'll be in charge here?"

"Just go!" the sheriff snapped. "Get started. I'll be out there myself in a little while."

"I'm goin!" the deputy said, and started for the door, then stopped. "Why does that guy call himself 'Lincoln's Avenger' anyway?"

"I don't have any idea," the sheriff said. "Now go."

# TWO

Clint Adams had spent a lot of time in Kansas over the years but, oddly, not a lot in Topeka. He knew that the Atchison, Topeka and Santa Fe Railroad had set up some shops in Topeka in 1878, and that the town—or city—had undergone a boom since then. Property was the most important commodity, with empty lots going for big money as investors got ready for other large businesses to move in. Clint didn't know if that was going to happen or not, but the population of Topeka had begun to grow by leaps and bounds, and it showed as he rode down Main Street. The streets were bulging with both pedestrian traffic, a wide variety of wagons and buckboards, as well as men on horseback.

He spotted a saloon and decided that a cold beer should be the first thing on his agenda. After that he'd find a livery for Eclipse, and a hotel for himself.

He entered the Jackpot Saloon and found a spot at the crowded bar. Since Topeka was also the state capital, a lot of the conversation that went on around him had to do with politics. He wasn't really interested in that, but when he

heard a snatch of another kind of conversation his ears
pricked up.

"Did you hear," someone asked, "that looney who thinks
he's 'Lincoln's Avenger' escaped from the hospital?"

"Who says?" another voice asked.

"The deputy," the first man said. "He's goin' around town
lookin' for a posse."

"For what?" the other asked. "To bring a crazy man back
to the hospital? That ain't any of our jobs."

"Why's he called 'Lincoln's Avenger' anyway?" the first
man asked.

"Damned if I know."

If they were talking about the man he thought they were
talking about, Clint knew. But he had to be sure.

He finished his beer, then left the Jackpot and went in
search of the deputy.

If the deputy was out looking to round up a posse, then
he was on the move. Topeka was too big for Clint to just
run into him. After an hour he decided to go, instead, to the
sheriff's office and see what he could find out there.

Sheriff Pete McKay sat behind his desk, fuming because
he had to track down an escaped patient from the mental
hospital. Why didn't the hospital have their own security
for that? McKay figured he should've told the director to
track the man down himself, but he took his job too seriously
for that. As long as the escapee could be a danger to someone, it was his responsibility to go out and bring him back.

When the door to his office opened, he expected to see
his deputy with some men for a posse. It was about time,
since he was just about to go out looking himself. Instead, it
was a man he'd never seen before.

                        *   *   *

As Clint entered, the man behind the desk asked, "Can I help you?"

"Are you the sheriff?"

"McKay is my name," the sheriff said. "And you?"

"Clint Adams."

McKay obviously recognized the name right away. Clint figured he would. McKay was in his forties, and was probably an experienced lawman.

"Mr. Adams," he said, with respect, "what brings you to Topeka? Not trouble, I hope."

"I hope not, too," Clint said. "I'm just passing through, Sheriff, but I hear you have a problem."

"Where did you hear that?"

"You mind if I sit down?"

"No, not at all," McKay said. "I'd offer you some coffee, but I don't have any made. I've been out."

"I heard some men talking over at the Jackpot Saloon about this situation."

"What did they have to say?"

"That you were trying to get up a posse to track down an escaped prisoner?"

"An escaped patient," McKay said, "from the mental hospital just outside of town."

"A mental patient?"

"That's right."

"Is he dangerous?"

"According to the director of the hospital, no," McKay said, "but he's not in his right mind. To me that makes him dangerous."

"I heard that this man has a nickname."

"Nickname," McKay repeated. "Well, yeah, but we're not sure who gave it to him. It might be he just calls himself that."

"And that name would be . . ."

"Lincoln's Avenger."

"See," Clint said, "I knew of a man by that name, once."

"That's odd," the sheriff said. "What was his real name?"

"Boston Corbett."

McKay took a slip of paper from his shirt pocket, looked at the name he had written on it when the director told it to him.

"Boston Corbett," he read. "That's it, all right. Do you think it's the same man you knew?"

"I don't know," Clint said. "It's not a very common name. Would you mind if I rode out to the hospital and found out?"

"I don't mind," McKay said, "but what's on your mind? I mean, if you find out it's the same man?"

"I'd be interested in helping you bring him back," Clint said, "alive."

"Well . . . I'd welcome your help, sir," McKay said. "You can ride out there tonight. I'm not sure the director will see you, though. He's not very cooperative."

"He'll see me," Clint said, standing up.

"You're not gonna cause any trouble, are you?" the sheriff asked. "I mean, I'd hate like hell to get called out there—"

"You won't," Clint said. "Like I said when I walked in, I'm not looking for trouble."

"Well, go ahead, then," McKay said. "Go and see if this man is your friend."

"He's not exactly a friend," Clint said, "just somebody I knew . . . somebody I've come across twice before."

"Is that a fact?"

"If it's the same man," Clint said, "and I'm kind of hop-

ing it isn't. I'd hate to think he ended up in a mental hospital . . . and yet I'm not surprised."

"You know," McKay said, "I think I'll ride out there
with you. It might make things easier for you."

"I'd be obliged."

McKay got up, grabbed his hat.

"My deputy is out lookin' for posse members," McKay
said, "but if you're willin' to help, I think maybe you and
me would be enough to bring him back. Then I could leave
my deputy behind. And I wouldn't have to worry about
some trigger-happy shopkeeper."

"Suits me."

They walked to the door together. Outside, the sheriff
said, "Just one thing."

"What's that?"

"The nickname," the sheriff said. "What's this thing
about 'Lincoln's Avenger'?"

"Well, Sheriff," Clint said, "if it's the same Boston Corbett, he avenged the death of Abraham Lincoln. He's the
man who shot John Wilkes Booth."

# THREE

When they reached the hospital, they tied their horses up outside and tried to enter the building. The door was locked. The sheriff knocked. An orderly, in his thirties, dressed in white, opened the door.

"I'm sorry, Sheriff," he said, "but visiting hours are—"

"I don't want to visit a patient," Sheriff McKay said. "I want to see the director."

"Well, he's not in his office. I'd have to bother him at home—"

"You do that," the sheriff said. He pushed his way in, followed by Clint. "This is Clint Adams. He also wants to see the director. Would you tell him that, please?"

"Clint . . . Adams?" the orderly asked.

"Yes. You know the name?"

"I, uh, do, yes," the man said. "I'll— I'll let the director know."

Sheriff McKay turned to look at Clint.

"I hope you don't mind me using your name," he said. "I thought it would get us in."

"That's okay."

Clint looked around. They were in a large entry foyer. From outside, the building just looked like a mansion, a huge private home.

"Yeah," the sheriff said, "this used to be a private home. It was sold a couple of years ago, and set up as this . . . this sanatorium."

"How many patients are here?"

"I don't know."

"Are any of them violent?"

"I don't know that, either," McKay said. "I don't know much about the place, really."

"Well," Clint said, "maybe we should find out some things about it today. Where does this director live?"

"There's a small house behind this one, used to be home to a caretaker. Now the director lives there."

"Maybe we should have gone there."

"No," the lawman said, "the rear of the property is fenced in. We had to come in this way."

The orderly returned.

"The director will see you in his office," he said. "Follow me, please."

They followed the orderly down a long corridor until they got to a closed door. The man knocked and opened it, then allowed Clint and the sheriff to go in.

"Sheriff," the director said, from behind his desk. He was a big, florid-faced man in his sixties. "I didn't think I'd see you again today."

"It's not me who wanted to see you, Mr. Desmond," the sheriff said. "This is Clint Adams. He wanted to talk to you about your escaped patient. Adams, this is Mr. Henry Desmond, the director of the Edgewood Sanatorium."

"We are the Edgewood Asylum, Mr. Adams," Desmond said, correcting the sheriff.

"What's the difference?" the sheriff said.

"There's a big difference, Sheriff," Desmond said. "The word 'asylum' means safe haven. A sanatorium is an institution. This is a place where people can feel safe while they are recovering from what ails them."

"Is that what Boston Corbett felt, Mr. Desmond?" Clint asked. "Safe?"

"What do you know about Boston Corbett, Mr. Adams?" Desmond asked.

"Well, if he's the same man, I knew him," Clint said. "And I know his background."

"I doubt there is more than one man named Boston Corbett," Desmond said. "What do you know about him?"

"Well, I know he was a soldier back when Lincoln was shot," Clint said. "And I know he's the man who shot and killed John Wilkes Booth."

"Really?" Desmond asked. "You mean . . . that was true?"

"Oh yes," Clint said. "Very true."

"So when he called himself 'Lincoln's Avenger'—" Desmond started, but Clint cut him off.

"He didn't call himself that," Clint said. "The newspapers gave him that name."

"I see."

"Does this make a difference, Mr. Desmond?" the sheriff asked.

"A difference how, Sheriff?"

"Do you want him back now?"

"Why would we want him back? He broke out, ran off,"

Desmond said. "Oh, I suppose I'll have to talk to the doctors, though."

"You're not a doctor?" Clint asked.

"No, I'm the director of this facility," Desmond said. "My job is to keep it running, and keep it funded."

"So it'll be up to a doctor whether Boston comes back here or not?" Clint asked.

"Oh, I suppose . . ."

"The man was a hero, Mr. Desmond," Clint said. "As far as I'm concerned, he's still a hero."

"Perhaps," the sheriff said, "but he's a disturbed one."

"Then he needs help," Desmond said. "He might actually be better off in a sanatorium, gentlemen, than here. But again, we can leave that up to the doctors."

"Then when we find him, we can bring him back here?" Clint asked.

"Yes, of course. You must bring him back here . . . if he's a hero."

After the orderly saw Clint Adams and Sheriff McKay out, the director grabbed a piece of paper, a quill pen, a blotter, and a bottle of ink. He proceeded to write a letter that, when completed, he would have messengered to the governor of the state so that it would get to him before Adams and the sheriff returned.

If he had his way, Boston Corbett would never see the inside of Edgewood again.

# FOUR

"What do you think?" Clint asked.

They were riding back to town.

"I don't think he ever wants to see Boston Corbett again," the sheriff said.

"Yeah, that's what I think."

"So he'll probably try to do somethin' to block us from bringin' Corbett back here."

"Something like what?"

McKay shrugged. "Pull strings?"

"Like, with a politician?"

"That's what he does."

"So he'll get in touch with a congressman, a senator, maybe even the governor of the state."

"I'll bet."

"And tell them what, I wonder?"

"I don't know," McKay said, "but it'll definitely be somethin' to get them on his side."

"Do you know where the director is from, Sheriff?" Clint asked.

"I'm not sure," the lawman said, "but I think it's some-where . . . in the South."

"Now, why doesn't that surprise me?"

By the time they reached Topeka, Clint had agreed to ride with Sheriff McKay to find Boston Corbett and bring him back.

"I'll get us outfitted and we can leave in the mornin'," McKay said. "I know your reputation, Adams, but how are you as a tracker?"

"Fair to middlin'," Clint said, "and I think you better start callin' me Clint, Sheriff."

"Okay, Clint."

"And for now," Clint added, "I'll just keep calling you Sheriff."

"Suit yourself," McKay said.

They unsaddled their horses at the livery, and McKay said, "I hope my horse can keep up with that monster of yours."

"Your gelding looks strong," Clint said. "It's not going to be a race."

As they left the livery, Clint said, "Can I buy you a drink?"

"At the Jackpot, later," McKay said. "I've got to head off my deputy, see if he's recruited any posse members. If he has, I'll have to go and unrecruit them."

"All right," Clint said. "I'll be at the Jackpot for a while."

"Like I said," McKay replied, "I'll see to our provisions."

"Let's travel light, Sheriff," Clint said. "Coffee and jerky's all I need. And I have my own guns, obviously."

"Okay," the sheriff said, "we'll travel light. I'll see you at the Jackpot in a couple of hours."

"I'll have to get a hotel room, and something to eat."

"Go to the Kansan Hotel, tell 'em to give you a room on the city," McKay said, as they walked away from the livery together. "The desk clerk should be a woman named Billie. Tell her she can check with me if she wants. Then have a steak in their dining room. It'll be pretty good."

When they got back to Main Street, they split up. Clint went directly to the Kansan Hotel. There was a pretty brown-haired woman behind the desk, about thirty.

"Welcome to the Kansan," she said. "Can I get you a room?"

"Yes, please," Clint said. He put his saddlebags and rifle down on top of the desk. "Sheriff McKay sent me over. He said the city would pay for my room. You can check with him, if you want."

"Are you working for the sheriff?"

"I'm going to ride out with him tomorrow."

"To bring back Boston Corbett?"

"How did you know?"

"It's all over town that he's trying to get up a posse," she said.

"Not anymore," Clint said. "It'll just be him and me."

She frowned.

"How do I know you're telling me the truth?" she asked.

"He told me to ask for Billie. Is that you?"

A stern look came over her face.

"My name is Wilhemina," she said. "Pete McKay is the only one who ever calls me Billie. He thinks it's funny."

"Well, it suits you," Clint said.

"Well, I guess he sent you over, all right," she said. She turned the register around. "Write your name in there and I'll give you Room Three."

"I hope your dining room is still open," Clint said. "McKay said I could get a good steak there."

"Well, he's right about that," she said. "Would you like me to have someone take your saddlebags to your room while you eat?"

"No, that's okay," Clint said. "I need to wash up. I've kind of been on the go all day."

"There should be water in the pitcher," she said. "If you want a bath, we can arrange that."

"I think I'll put that off," Clint said. "I could use one, but I'll be back on the trail tomorrow, anyway."

"That's up to you . . . ," she turned the register back around so she could read it, ". . . Mr. Adams. Here's your key." If she recognized his name, she gave no sign.

"Thank you."

"Second floor, to the right," she said.

He took his saddlebags and rifle and went up the stairs to the second floor.

# FIVE

Sheriff McKay found his deputy, Paul Gaines, in the office.

"There ya are, Sheriff," Gaines said. "I got bad news. The only men willin' to ride in a posse ain't the kind I wanna go out on the trail with."

"That's okay, Paul," McKay said. "We got a change of plans."

McKay stared at the deputy until the man got out of his chair so the sheriff could sit behind his own desk.

"What's goin' on, Sheriff?" Gaines asked.

"I'll be goin' out to find the patient on my own, with one man along."

"Just you and me?" Gaines asked. "That suits me, but who's gonna be in charge—"

"No, not you and me, Paul," McKay said. "You're gonna stay here and be in charge."

"Me? But . . . who's gonna ride with ya?"

"Clint Adams."

"Clint . . . the Gunsmith?"

"That's right."

"When did he get to town?"

"Today, as a matter of fact."

"B-but . . . why would he wanna go out with ya?"

"Because he knows the patient," McKay said. "His name is Boston Corbett."

"Boston—what kinda name is that?"

"A famous one, apparently," McKay said. "And for more than shooting up the House of Representatives. He's supposed to be some kind of hero."

"Hero? For doin' what?"

"He's the man who shot John Wilkes Booth."

"John Wilkes . . . who?"

McKay glared at the younger man.

"Brush up on your history, boy," he said. "John Wilkes Booth is the man who assassinated Abraham Lincoln."

"Ohhh! But that was a long time ago."

"The man is still a hero if he shot the man who killed Abe Lincoln, don't you think?"

"I . . . guess."

"You guess," McKay said. "Look, go out and tell your posse members we ain't gonna need them, after all."

"Well, okay."

"And what's your problem? You been wantin' me to leave you in charge for a long time. Well, now you get your chance."

"Oh, that's right," Gaines said, perking up. "Well . . . okay, then."

"Go!" McKay said.

The deputy left and McKay leaned back in his chair. He wondered if he and Adams would be able to get out of town in the morning before somebody from the new Topeka Police Department found out what was going on.

* * *

Director Desmond called his assistant in and handed him two envelopes. One was addressed to the governor of the state, the other to the chief of police in Topeka.

"See to it that these are hand-delivered," he said.

"The governor?" the man said, surprised.

"Yes, the governor," Desmond said. "Just see that they're delivered as soon as possible, Willis."

"Today, sir?" Willis asked. "But it's gettin' late. The governor won't be at the capitol building—"

"Have it delivered to his home," Desmond said. "The same with the police chief." He put his hand up. "No more questions, Willis. Just do it!"

"Yes, sir."

As Willis left his office, Desmond sat back in his chair. He knew both the governor and the police chief would be of a similar mind with him. He just hoped they'd react quickly, and correctly.

---

The room was satisfactory, as was the steak. The coffee was bad, very weak, but he had to have coffee, so he drank it.

After he ate, Clint left the hotel and walked over to the Jackpot. The place was busy, men standing shoulder-to-shoulder at the bar, girls working the floor. There were no gaming tables, but that didn't mean there was no gambling going on. Clint could hear shouts of both elation and pain as the cards went one way or the other. This wasn't a night for him to play poker, though, so he went to the bar to see if he could muscle his way in.

---

The governor of the state of Kansas looked up from the book he was reading as his wife entered the study.

"Darling, a man dropped this off at the door for you," she said, extending an envelope to him.

He frowned, taking it from her.

"Why didn't he just deliver it to me tomorrow at work?" he wondered.

"It looks like it's from that annoying man Desmond, who runs that hospital."

"Hmm," the governor said, "they had an escapee from there earlier today."

"I wish they'd get them all out of there," she said, with a shudder. "I hate having that place so close to town."

He'd been listening to her whine about one thing or another for forty years.

"All right, dear," he said, "I'll take care of this. Why don't you go and have some of your medicine?"

"I think I will," she said, leaving the room.

Her "medicine" was whiskey, and the more she had, the sooner she'd fall asleep, and the sooner he could slip his mistress in through the back door.

He sighed, sat back in his chair, let the book sit in his lap, and opened the envelope. What he found inside was quite interesting.

The chief of police was working late that night, so when the man came with the envelope from Director Desmond, he found the chief behind his desk.

"Chief?" he said. "They sent me up here with this."

"Who sent you up here?" the big man demanded.

"Uh, the man at the front desk."

The chief shook his head. If this man was so inclined, he could have pulled a gun and shot the chief dead behind his desk. Something was going to have to be done about the security of this building.

"All right, thank you."

The messenger left. Chief Paul Nolan sat back in his

chair and opened the envelope, took out the missive, and read it. Seeing who it was from, he was sure a similar letter had been sent to the governor. That meant he was going to have to take some kind of action. Both Desmond and the governor were Southerners, and for Southerners the damn war was never over.

He rose from the desk and walked to his door. He looked out at his aide's desk. Lieutenant Cooper was not there, which was no surprise. He saw a sergeant walking by and shouted, "Sergeant!"

"Yes, sir!"

"Find me Lieutenant Cooper."

"Uh, it's late, sir. He may have gone home."

Shit, Chief Nolan thought. He'd forgotten how late it was.

"I don't care," he said. "Find him, and if he's home, get him here!"

"Yes, sir."

The chief went back into his office, and this time he slammed the door. Maybe whoever does come up here to kill me, he thought, will at least knock.

# SIX

Boston Corbett awoke that morning with a start, sat up, and stared around himself with wide eyes.

Where was he?

Where was his uniform?

And his rifle?

He tried to concentrate. Were they still searching for John Wilkes Booth, or had he already shot the assassin of Abraham Lincoln? He could remember it like it was yesterday—or a few minutes ago.

It was April 24, 1865, when he was selected as one of twenty-six cavalrymen to pursue Booth. It took two days, but on April 26 they managed to corner him in a barn in Virginia. Boston remembered the smell of tobacco. There was another man with him, as well, but Boston was only concerned with Booth. He crept close to the barn, then right up to it, so he could see through the slats of one wall. He took out his pistol, poked it through the slats, and fired one shot. The bullet hit John Wilkes Booth in the side of the neck.

Mortally wounded, Booth would eventually expire while lying there on the ground.

Boston came back to himself, stood up, and looked around. Now he remembered. He wasn't in Virginia. He was in Kansas. He'd escaped from the hospital, where they had branded him as mentally unstable. He wasn't unstable. He got confused sometimes, but that was natural.

Wasn't it?

He needed two things—some food and a horse. Which was more pressing changed with the gnawing in his belly. He knew from experience that you could get past that point of starvation, that point when it felt like something was trying to dig its way out of your belly. He was past that point now; the hunger had been pushed back. So now the urgency he felt was for a horse.

A horse . . .

Some new clothes . . .

A gun . . .

And then some food.

The sun was coming up. He knew somebody would be coming after him. Probably a lawman. He was fully awake now, and not so confused.

He knew what to do.

He had to keep moving.

# SEVEN

When Clint woke up, there was a girl in his bed. He must have been really tired, because he wasn't drunk last night, and yet he still couldn't remember bringing a girl back to his room with him.

She rolled onto her back at that point. The sheet was down to her waist, so the first thing he saw was a very nice pair of full breasts, with dark brown nipples. Very pretty! Then he looked at her face and was surprised to see that the girl in his bed was actually a woman—Billie, the desk clerk of the hotel.

He sat up and tried to wake himself up. He looked down at his crotch. Well, at least one part of him was awake. That was what a nice pair of breasts could do for you in the morning.

Billie moaned in her sleep, then turned her back to him, showing that her ass was as nicely shaped and padded as her breasts.

Well, he thought, she was there, he was there, they must

have gotten there together, so it wouldn't be a shock to her if he touched her.

He rolled over, pulled the sheet down just a bit more, then pressed his swollen cock to the cleft between her ass cheeks. Her butt was so well muscled that the crease there was deep enough to take hold of him.

He began to move against her, rubbing himself up and down her butt crease. She moaned again, pressed back against him, then opened her legs. She reached behind her to take hold of him and slide him up between her thighs. Then she moved her hand, reached between her thighs for him, and pressed him against her pussy, which was already wet, leading him to believe she'd been awake longer than she let on.

Or she'd been having a really good dream.

Sheriff McKay made an early visit to the general store and told the storekeeper he'd be by soon to pick up the supplies. After that he walked to his office and let himself in. He was annoyed that the deputy was not there yet. This was the man he was going to leave in charge when he left town with Clint Adams?

He made coffee, and was still having second thoughts about his deputy when the door opened and Lieutenant Eric Cooper of the Topeka Police Department came in. Of everybody in that department, this was the only man McKay could stomach. He was the only policeman who didn't treat him like he was eighty years old.

"Mornin', Sheriff," Cooper said.

"Lieutenant Cooper," McKay said. "Word gets around fast."

"What word?" Cooper walked to the coffeepot and poured himself a cup.

"Boston Corbett?"

Cooper sat down across from the sheriff. He was in his late thirties, and McKay knew Cooper had spent years wearing a badge before he joined the Topeka department and was immediately given the rank of lieutenant.

"Come on, Coop," McKay said. "I know Desmond must've sent word to your boss, and probably to everyone's boss, the governor, as soon as he found out that his patient really was 'Lincoln's Avenger.'"

"And who told you and the director that Boston Corbett really was 'Lincoln's Avenger'?" Cooper asked.

"A man who knew him then," the sheriff said. "Clint Adams."

Cooper tried to look unconcerned as he sipped his coffee.

"The Gunsmith," he said. "I heard he was in town. What's his interest?"

"He wants to make sure that Corbett is returned safely," McKay said. "He and I are ridin' out today to start lookin'."

"He could be anywhere by now."

"Not if he's on foot," McKay said. "He might not have gone far."

"When are you leaving?"

"Any minute."

"I have bad news," Cooper said.

"For who?" McKay asked. "You or me?"

"For both of us, actually," Cooper said. "I'm coming with you."

"That is bad news," McKay said. "Orders from on high?"

"From Chief Nolan."

"Ah! Anybody heard from the governor yet?"

"I don't know, Sheriff. All I know is the chief has ordered me to assist you in your hunt."

"I don't think we need any help, Lieutenant," the sheriff said. "I think Clint Adams and I can handle it just fine without you."

"Well, be that as it may," Cooper said, "I'm coming. I've got my gun, my rifle, my horse is outside. What are we doing for provisions?"

"Traveling light," McKay said. "Coffee and beef jerky. That's it."

"Not even a few cans of beans?"

"Beans mean bringing a pan, and some plates, and spoons or forks," McKay said. Maybe if he made it sound bad enough, the man would change his mind. Except that McKay knew Cooper well enough to know he would follow his orders, no matter what.

"Well, where's your new partner?" Cooper asked.

"Probably still at the hotel."

"Why don't we go and meet him there? I'll bet he's having breakfast before we leave."

"The dining room probably isn't open," McKay said, "but that might not be a bad idea."

"What about his horse?" Cooper asked. "Maybe we could saddle it for him."

"I wouldn't touch his horse without his say-so," McKay said. "When you see it, you'll know why."

He got up, and both lawmen left the office together.

# EIGHT

Clint got Billie on her knees, got onto his knees behind her, and started fucking her from there. She started slamming her big butt back into him, so that the room filled with the sound of her flesh slapping against his.

She pulled away from him then, flipped herself onto her back, and spread her legs wide for him, holding onto her own ankles.

"Like this," she gasped, "come on, come on . . ."

She didn't have to invite him twice. He got between her legs, but instead of driving his cock into her, it was his tongue. She caught her breath as he avidly lapped at her, biting and licking and sucking until she was gushing onto his face, writhing on the bed, soaking the sheets, her thighs, and his face. He found the scent of her intoxicating and only stopped when she pushed him away with a loud groan.

"You're killin' me!" she said. "God! Come on, come on, I want you in me!"

Clint knew the sheriff might be coming for him at any moment, and he had to be ready, so he jammed his cock

into her this time and began to just pound away at her. He
hated to do it, but he had to end it as soon as possible, so he
chased his own orgasm . . .

He left Billie in his room, in the bed, complaining that
she needed sleep because he hadn't let her sleep all night.
He didn't dare tell her that he still didn't remember what
had happened during the night. Maybe he did come back
from the saloon drunk, see her behind the desk, and drag
her back to his room. She didn't really seem to mind, except to complain about the lack of sleep.

He went down to the lobby, intending to leave and col-
lect his horse, but he noticed that the dining room was
open, and smelled the scent of frying steak. He was stuck
for a decision when the sheriff entered with another man.

"I was just going to go get my horse," Clint said. "Who's
this?"

"Dining room's open," McKay observed. "Why don't I
tell you about this here fella over breakfast, and then you
can go and get your horse—I mean, seein' as how we're
gonna be traveling light and all."

"Suits me," Clint said. "Come on."

Over steak and eggs Sheriff McKay introduced Lieutenant
Cooper to Clint Adams.

"Why didn't the police department show an interest before?" Clint asked.

"I can't answer that," Cooper said. "I got my orders last
night."

"Take a guess," Clint suggested.

Cooper looked at McKay, who shrugged.

"The fact that there was a patient out there who was
called, or called himself, 'Lincoln's Avenger,' was not a

secret," Cooper said, "but nobody actually believed the man had earned that name."

"So now it makes a difference?" Clint asked.

"To some people, I guess so."

"You know the director out there, Desmond?"

"I've met him."

"He's a Southerner, isn't he?"

"I don't know that, Mr. Adams."

"What about your chief?" Clint asked. "Is he a Southerner?"

"I think he is."

"So to a Southerner 'Lincoln's Avenger' must take on a whole different meaning, wouldn't you say?"

"I say the war was over a long time ago, Mr. Adams," Cooper replied.

"Come on, Cooper," Clint said, "you know as well as I do that for the losing side, no war is ever over."

Cooper leaned forward and looked straight into Clint's eyes.

"If you think I'm bein' sent along with you as some sort of assassin, think again, mister. That's not what I do."

"I didn't say that."

"You were gettin' there."

The two men eyed each other, and then McKay broke the silence.

"Okay, whatever the reason," he said, "it looks like the three of us are going after him together. Let's not get off on the wrong foot here."

Cooper leaned back, picked up his coffee cup, and drained it. Clint did the same.

"We done here?" McKay asked. "I think it's time for us to mount up and get movin'."

# NINE

They agreed to meet in front of the general store after Clint retrieved Eclipse from the livery stable. Cooper stuck with McKay. He didn't like to admit it, even to himself, but he was intimidated by Clint Adams. But he was going to have to go out of his way not to show it.

"What are ya doin'?" McKay asked him as they walked their mounts over to the store.

"What do you mean?"

"Are ya tryin' to rile him up?"

"He doesn't scare me," Cooper said.

"Then you're stupid," McKay said, "because he scares the hell outta me."

"Why do we need him, anyway?"

"Well, first," McKay said, "I didn't know there was gonna be a we. And second, he knows the man."

"If it's the same man."

"How many Boston Corbett's could there be?" McKay asked.

Reluctantly, Cooper said, "Maybe you're right."

"Yeah, I know I'm right," McKay said, "and if it ain't the same man, the chief and the governor and even Adams are gonna be pretty disappointed."

When they reached the general store, Cooper waited outside with the horse while McKay went inside for their supplies. When he came out with a single burlap sack, Cooper said, "That's it?"

"That's all Adams wants to take," McKay said.

"Why does he get to say what we bring?" Cooper complained.

"Well, as I said before," McKay patiently repeated, "I didn't know there was going to be a we, and second . . . he's Clint Adams."

"You're giving him too much respect."

"And you're not givin' him enough," McKay said. "Look, can you track?"

"I'm no tracker," Cooper said. "Never was. That's why you're a better sheriff than I ever was."

"Well, that may be, but I'm no tracker, either," McKay said. "So we're gonna need Adams to track this man. I'm askin' you not to antagonize him."

"Fine," Cooper said, "but you've got to tell him that I'm in charge."

"Why would I do that?" McKay asked. "You ain't in charge."

"The police department supersedes the sheriff's office," McKay said.

"I ain't sure I know what supersedes means," McKay said, "but it don't sound like somethin' I'd like. Look, I went out to the hospital and took the report, I signed Adams up for this hunt, so I'm the one who's in charge."

"I'm a lieutenant—"

"That don't matter to me, Coop," McKay said. "You

know that. If it did, I woulda joined the police department, too."

"You could've," Cooper said, "as a sergeant."

"Yeah, you'd like that, wouldn't ya?" McKay said. "Then you would be in charge, wouldn't ya?"

"Look, Sheriff—"

"What are you two fighting about?" Clint asked.

They both turned and stared at him. He and his horse had come up on them so quietly that neither man had heard them. They both wondered how he had done that.

"Nothin'," McKay said, "we ain't fightin' over nothin'.' In fact, we ain't fightin'."

"Fine," Clint said. "Since you're done not fighting, are we ready to go?"

"I got the supplies," McKay said. "Beef jerky and coffee, like you said."

"I've got a coffeepot."

"Oh," McKay said, because he'd forgotten that, "well, good."

"Let's get mounted up and moving, then," Clint said.

"I suggest we pick up his trail right from the hospital building."

"Good idea," McKay said, mounting up.

Cooper mounted up, and kept silent. The three men rode out of town together, and Clint wondered just how well this partnership was going to go.

# TEN

They rode out to the hospital, and instead of talking with the director, Clint decided—or suggested—they speak with one of the orderlies. They managed to find a man, named Leland, who was willing to talk to them, and walk them through Boston Corbett's escape route.

"He came through these doors," the man said, walking them along, "then out this door—"

"How did he get past the locks?" Cooper asked.

"That's a good question," Leland said. He was a tall, thin man in his thirties, with a fringe of graying hair around a bald pate. "He either had some kind of key, or figured out how to pick the locks."

"What would he use?" Clint asked. "Weren't sharp objects kept away from him?"

"Yes, but he could have stolen a knife or a fork—" Leland started.

"You can't pick a lock with a knife or a fork," Cooper said.

"Maybe not," Clint said, inspecting one of the doors, "but he could slip one. See? There's enough room to get a knife in here and slip that lock open."

They continued on until they got to the outside.

"Once he was out this door, he was free to just . . . light out."

"On foot, right?"

"We only have one horse here. It's used for the director's buggy, and that horse is still here, so yeah, he's gotta be on foot," Leland explained. "At least, he started out that way."

Clint looked out at the ground in front of them. For the foreseeable distance it seemed to be a grassy field, but he knew that wouldn't last. The ground would get hard and unyielding. If he was an escapee, he'd look for a horse as soon as possible.

"I don't think we're going to be able to track him very far if he's on foot," Clint said.

"Why not?" Cooper asked.

"Once the ground gets hard he's not going to leave much sign for us to follow, not the way a horse would. And besides, I think he's going to steal a horse as soon as he can."

"From where?" Cooper asked.

"That's a question for the sheriff to answer," Clint said.

"What direction?" McKay asked.

"Let's go and find out."

Clint found the footpath left by the escapee. Even after all this time, the grass and brush he'd trampled down were still evident.

Eventually they reached a tree line and had to mount up. Broken branches and stepped-on twigs still enabled him to track the man, but after a few hours they finally came to some hard ground.

Clint reined Eclipse in and looked at the other two men. Sheriff McKay appeared natural in the saddle, but Lieutenant Cooper had obviously been out of the saddle for some time. He was sitting gingerly on his horse.

"Let's dismount," Clint said. "I want to walk around a bit."

McKay stepped down, and did not notice the relief on Cooper's face as he dismounted and surreptitiously rubbed his butt with both hands.

Clint saw it, though. He gave the man time to rub life back into his hindquarters, then returned to where the two men were standing.

"Okay, Sheriff," Clint asked, "what's east of here?"

"You're talkin' about some place he could get a horse?" McKay asked.

"That's right."

"Well, a couple of small towns, a few ranches—"

"Big spreads?" Clint asked.

"No," McKay said, "nothin' very big."

"And the towns? Large towns?"

"No," McKay said, "definitely small towns."

"Just because he's walking east now doesn't mean he'll continue," Cooper said. "Especially if he's out of his head."

"Even if he's out of his head, he's going to walk in a straight line," Clint said.

"That don't make sense," McKay said, then looked at Cooper. "Does it?"

Cooper shrugged.

"Any man on foot, no matter how crazy, is going to look for a horse," Clint said. "He'll keep to a straight line until he finds one. Then he may acquire a little imagination."

"I suppose you're speaking from experience?" Cooper asked.

"I am."

"Can't exactly argue with that," McKay said.

Clint waited to see if an argument would come from Cooper. When it didn't, they mounted up.

# ELEVEN

They were forced to camp for the night without any sign of Boston Corbett.

"He must've made damn good time on foot," McKay said, pouring out coffee for the three of them. They each had a piece of beef jerky in their hands. Cooper was the only one looking unhappy about it.

"Maybe he ran into a rider and stole their horse," Cooper said.

"We didn't encounter anyone," Clint said. "Plus, I don't think he'd be in any condition to overpower anyone and steal their horse. He's going to have to steal one by being sneaky."

"Well, we better find out tomorrow," Cooper said. "I ain't staying out here for days."

"It might take days to find him," McKay said, "maybe weeks."

"What are your orders?" Clint asked.

"To find him and bring him back."

"Is there a time limit?"

"No," Cooper said, through tightened lips.

"Well, Coop," McKay said, "you can go back anytime you want. We don't mind."

Cooper bit viciously into his beef jerky.


In the middle of the night Clint was sitting at the fire when McKay came up behind him.

"You standin' watch?" he asked. "No reason for that."

"No, just couldn't sleep," Clint said.

"Why not?"

"Just thinking."

"About what?"

"Boston Corbett," Clint said. "He's had kind of a hard life for a hero."

"Yeah, so I understand," McKay said. "I wonder why that is."

"Well, for one thing," Clint said, "not everybody thought he was a hero. There were a lot of people who thought that he was the assassin."

"Southerners."

"Mostly."

"Musta been hard on him."

"It was," Clint said, "but he was also his own worst enemy. Got himself in trouble, almost went to prison, until the secretary of war stepped in and said he should be treated as a hero. I'm afraid killing Booth was the high point of Boston Corbett's life."

"How did you meet him?" McKay asked. "And when? Before or after he shot Booth?"

"I met him after," Clint said, "but I was in Washington when Lincoln was shot. In fact, I was staying in the rooming house where they brought him afterward . . ."

# TWELVE

Clint was a young man when he got to Washington, D.C., in April of 1865, but he already had a reputation across the country. The legend of "The Gunsmith" had been born several years earlier in newspapers in both the East and the West, not to mention the North and South.

He had spent the last year of the war doing some work for Allan Pinkerton, then operating as head of Lincoln's new Secret Service under the name E. J. Allan. Pinkerton wanted to be able to go back to his business as a private detective after the war, and didn't wish the world at large to know what he had been doing during the conflict.

But Clint stayed in Washington only to celebrate the end of the war, to enjoy what the city of Washington had to offer in the way of eat, drink, gambling, and women, before he returned to his beloved West.

He had taken a room at Peterson's Boardinghouse, across the street from Ford's Theater. Earlier in the day he'd had his final meeting with "E. J. Allan," at a restaurant near the White House.

"You're late," Pinkerton had said.

Clint had noticed that no matter what he did he annoyed Allan Pinkerton.

"Technically," Clint said, sitting down, "I don't work for you anymore."

"You're an arrogant young man," Pinkerton said, "and I doubt that will ever change."

"It will," Clint assured him. "Eventually I'll be an arrogant older man, like you."

"I'm only forty-six years old!"

"Really? That old?"

A waiter arrived, which kept Pinkerton from lashing out at Clint.

"Steak with everything," Clint said.

"For lunch?"

"You're paying, right?"

"Yes." Actually, the government was paying, but the difference wasn't worth discussing.

"Steak," Clint said, again, "with everything—and a beer."

The waiter looked at Pinkerton, who shook his head and said, "The same."

"Yes, sir, Mr. Allan," the man said.

"You still E. J. Allan?" Clint asked. "When does that stop?"

"When I go back to my agency."

"When will that be?"

"When the President no longer needs me."

"And how is the President these days?"

"Mr. Lincoln is fine," Pinkerton said "He and Mrs. Lincoln are going to Ford's Theater tonight to see some blasted new play."

"Ford's? I'm staying right across the street from there. Maybe I can look out my window and get a look at them."

"I tried to get him to reconsider, but he's almost as bull-headed and vexing as you are."

"I'll take that as a compliment," Clint said, "but 'vexing?'"

"Yes."

"You have him covered, don't you?"

"There will be soldiers in the theater, and John Parker, of the Metropolitan Police Force, will be in his box with him."

"That sounds like plenty of coverage."

"Unless he's the target of a lunatic, who doesn't care if he's killed."

"Are we here to talk about lunatics?"

"No," Pinkerton said, "we're here to talk about you."

"Me?"

"As I've said, as soon as the President doesn't need me anymore, I'll be going back to my business. I'll have offices in New York, Chicago, and somewhere in California—we're not sure where yet."

"Sounds good for you," Clint said.

"And maybe you."

"How do you mean?"

"I want you to come and work for me."

"Me?" Clint asked. "Be a Pinkerton man?"

"Why not?"

"Well," Clint said, "for one thing, I'm vexing."

"You are that," Pinkerton said. "You're also a good man, and the best hand with a gun I've ever seen." That would be the first and last time Allan Pinkerton ever graced him with a compliment.

"I'm not a detective."

"I have a man working for me named Talbot Roper. He's an excellent detective. He will teach you everything you need to know. You have a lot in common."

"Such as?"

"He's your age, and he's arrogant."

"Sounds like I'll like him."

"That really doesn't matter," Pinkerton said.

At that point the waiter arrived with their lunches and set their steaming plates down in front of them, followed by cold, deep glasses of beer.

"You can go to New York even before I do and get started—"

"Wait, wait," Clint said. "I've always been under the impression that you don't like me." He had almost said, "that we don't like each other," but he figured why antagonize the man who was paying for his meal.

"That is a correct impression," Pinkerton said. "What's that got to do with you working for me?"

"Well," Clint said, "there could be several answers to that, but I think I'll just pick one."

"And that is?"

"I don't want to work for you."

"Why not? I'll pay you well, and the work will be interesting."

"Don't take offense, Allan," Clint said, "but I don't want to work for anyone."

"So what do you want to do?" he asked. "Just go back to the West and be a layabout?"

"That's close," Clint said. "Not exactly a layabout, but I do want to travel . . . wander, however you want to put it. I'm going to be my own man."

Clint cut into his steak, tasted it, and said, "This is really good."

Pinkerton cut into his viciously, stuffed it into his mouth, and chewed furiously—which was fitting, because Clint knew it made him furious to be turned down.

# THIRTEEN

After lunch with Pinkerton, Clint had left the man still fuming and gone to see if he could find a game, or a girl.

He found them both.

He spent much of the afternoon playing poker. He wasn't very good at it, but it was his intention to become not only better, but excellent at it. On the afternoon in question, however, he paid for his lessons, losing to an older, very quiet man who only spoke when he had to.

Clint left the table and went to the bar for a beer. In all the hours he had played he had drunk nothing. That was a lesson he had learned earlier in his poker playing. He had been very hot one day, way ahead, and started to celebrate early, only to end up drunkenly losing all his profit, as well as his investment. It was a lesson he only had to be taught once.

The poker game had been in a separate room from the bar. In point of fact this was not a public establishment but a private club he had been invited to. There were not only men in the club, but women—for the most part, wives of members.

He noticed one woman watching him from a table as he

stood at the bar. She was a handsome woman in her early forties, sitting with a man who appeared to be in his sixties. He was laughing and having a conversation with two other men, ignoring her except to put a meaty hand on her knee from time to time—a gesture of ownership, no doubt.

She had hair the color of honey, a body that seemed long and lean as she sat there. She had a long, graceful neck and a wide smile he could see from across the room. Clint liked older women, and he had found over the past few years that they liked him. He'd learned a lot from them, and he took his lessons in poker and in sex very seriously.

He turned his back and leaned on the bar, figuring to reel her in. Another older woman had once cautioned him never to show too much interest. "Make them come to you, darling," she'd told him, "and believe me, they will."

He ordered a second beer, and watched the lady in the mirror behind the bar. He decided to give it until the end of this beer. She would only make a move if her husband got up and drifted away, perhaps to do some business.

Clint was just about finished, when he saw the man pat his wife's knee, get up, and walk away with two friends. Clint drained his mug, turned, and started to saunter toward the door. He stopped when he felt a hand on his arm.

"You're not leaving without me, are you?" she asked. "Not after all we've meant to each other."

He turned to look at her. Up close he saw that she was a little older than he had thought, but she was also beautiful rather than handsome.

"What about your husband?" he asked.

"Oh, he'll be busy for the rest of the night," she said. "He expects me to go home."

"By yourself?"

"Well," she said, "that will be up to you, won't it?"

"Ma'am," he said, "I ain't exactly going to go home with you."

"Well then," she said, linking her arm through his, "I guess I'll have to go home with you."

Mr. and Mrs. Lincoln were shown to their box in Ford's Theater. Mary Lincoln was very excited to see the performance of *Our American Cousin*. Major Henry Rathbone and his fiancée, Clara Harris, were seated with them. Lincoln had first invited General Grant and his wife to attend, but they had declined. Several others had declined, as well, until Major Rathbone accepted.

The door to the box was closed and locked, and John Parker took up a position right outside.

For all intents and purposes, the Lincolns were considered safe.

John Wilkes Booth handed his ticket to the ticket taker and was admitted to the theater. He was a well-known actor, had performed in many theaters, including this one, and knew exactly where the President's box was. He had also made other preparations. He had prepared a notched brace that would fit against the door perfectly, once he entered the box. No one would be able to break in once he was inside.

He had his gun in his belt, and he had secreted the notched brace near the box. All he had to do now was wait for the play to begin.

Clint managed to get himself and Mrs. Frieda Jenkins into his room at Peterson's Boardinghouse. Frieda's husband was an important banker in Washington, a man who was more married to his job than he was to her.

"He's also older than I am," she said, "so I'm usually left

to my own devices to find some, uh, satisfaction," she had told Clint in the cab.

She told him this in between kisses. As soon as the cab-driver closed the door and climbed up top, she was all over Clint, kissing him soundly while her hand slid down into his lap. Her kisses were avid, and exciting, and her hand on him just hastened things along.

"Oh, my," she said, "this is what I like about young men. You're already hard!"

"Well, you're an exciting woman, Frieda," he said.

She laughed.

"I'm an older woman," she said, "but you like older women, don't you, Clint?"

"I like beautiful women," he said, "and that's what you are."

"Ah, you're also a sweet-talker," she said. She kissed him again, deeply enough to leave them both breathless. "Sweet kisser, and a sweet-talker. You got anything else that's sweet?"

He laughed and said, "That's going to be for you to find out."

They got into his room without being seen and she came into his arms. She was tall and slender, as he had guessed while she was seated. He kissed her long, beautiful neck and she caught her breath. Her hand slid down between them and rubbed him.

"I've got to see," she said, getting down on her knees, "I've got to see, and taste. Do you mind?"

"Not at all," Clint said. "Help yourself."

"Oh," she said, undoing his trousers, "believe me, this is going to help me a lot. I had my eye on you as soon as you went to the bar tonight."

"Funny," he said, "that's about the same time I spotted you."

"I know," she said. "It sounds corny, but our eyes met across the room."

He was about to say something else but instead he gasped as she pulled him out of his pants and started licking him.

# FOURTEEN

Frieda had a marvelous body for a woman of her age. Lucky for her she had been lean all her life, so there was virtually no sag to her small breasts, no looseness in her belly. Her butt was smooth and muscular, her legs long and graceful.

She had no problem squatting in front of him, licking and sucking him for an extended period of time.

She spread his feet and placed his hands gently on her head, not holding, or even guiding, but just resting there.

While her head was bobbing back and forth on him, her hands were alternately squeezing his balls, kneading his butt, sliding up and down the backs of his thighs. She began to moan as she sucked him, while he strove for silence.

"You're so quiet," she said, releasing him for a moment. "Strong silent type?"

"Not usually," he said, "but we are in a rooming house, and I don't want to get kicked out . . . especially not now."

"Don't worry," she said. "I'm used to being quiet. I'm usually lying in my own bed, trying to stay quiet."

"You bring men into your bed while your husband's home?"

"No, men," she said, "just me."

His penis jumped as that picture formed in his head.

"Come on," he said. "This time you'll be in my bed."

He pulled her to her feet, guided her to the bed, and kissed her before he laid her down on her back. He got rid of the rest of his clothes, then climbed atop her, rubbing his face against her little breasts and hard nipples. This time it was she who held his head while he licked and bit her large, hard nipples. He slid one hand down between her thighs to tease her, and found her very wet.

"I'm ready," she whispered, "I am so ready."

He didn't make her wait. That would have been cruel. He lifted one leg over her, pressed his penis to her wet pussy, and slid himself in, slowly, until he was completely engulfed by her heat.

"Oh, yessss," she said, sibilantly. "Slow at first, please?"

He put his mouth next to her ear and assured her, "I'm in no hurry."

Across the street John Wilkes Booth was slipping into Lincoln's box, wielding both a gun and a knife. He pushed the notched brace against the door, effectively locking it, then moved forward. He held the gun out, almost against the back of Lincoln's head, and pulled the trigger. It was a small gun, but the theater was quiet at that moment and everyone heard the shot.

Major Rathbone turned and lunged at Booth immediately, but Booth used his knife and inflicted a gash on the young soldier's arm. Then Booth climbed up on the edge of the box and leaped to the stage. As he landed, he felt something in his ankle and knew he had injured himself. Nevertheless, he got to his feet, brandishing his knife so no one would try to stop him, and shouted, "*Sic semper tyrannis.*" Which meant "Thus always to tyrants."

He ran from the stage . . .

Realizing what had happened, a doctor named Charles Leale rushed to Lincoln's box, only to find the door locked tightly. He shouted at someone inside to let him in so he could help the President.

Inside, Major Rathbone, realizing the door was blocked, kicked away the brace while holding onto his bleeding arm. Dr. Leale rushed in and immediately began to examine the President, who had been shot in the back of the head.

Clint was grunting with the effort he was putting into slamming his penis in and out of Frieda's sopping pussy. As he did so, he became dimly aware of some commotion outside his closed window. It became so loud that even Frieda noticed it.

"What is going on?" she asked, breathily.

"I don't know," Clint said. He withdrew himself from her and rushed to the window. As he opened it, he heard someone shouting, "He's been shot, he's been shot!"

Someone came running by Clint's second-story window, and Clint shouted, "What's going on? Who's been shot?"

"Lincoln," a man said. "President Lincoln's been shot!"

# FIFTEEN

Clint grabbed his gun and said to Frieda, "Wait right here!"

He pulled on his pants and ran out of the room shirtless and bootless. When he got downstairs, William Peterson was there. Also another boarder, named Henry Safford.

"What's happened?"

"Lincoln's been shot!" Clint shouted.

When he got outside, people were milling about in the street between the boardinghouse and the theater.

"They're comin' out!" somebody shouted. "They're carryin' him out!"

People were both crowding to see Lincoln and trying to get out of the way so the wounded president could be carried out.

Carrying the President outside at all was an ill-conceived idea. Once they had him outside, no one knew what to do.

"Here!" Clint shouted. "Bring him here!"

"Yes," Henry Safford shouted behind him, "bring him in here." Safford was waving a lamp to get their attention.

Clint ran into the boardinghouse ahead of the men carrying Lincoln.

"Do you have an empty room?" he asked Peterson.

"Yes," the man said.

"Show them where."

"Here!" Peterson shouted, and led the way to a second-floor empty room.

They carried the President in and laid him on the bed. Clint found out later that among the men were three doctors who had been in the audience—Leale, King, and Taft. Clint and other boarders stood outside the room, waiting for word. People from the street had crowded in and were on the stairs and in the front room.

Frieda stayed in Clint's room so no one would see her, but she cracked the door and stared out. She was worried someone would recognize her, but she was even more worried about Mr. Lincoln.

One of the doctors came outside, shaking his head.

"How is he?" Clint demanded.

Dr. Leale looked at Clint and some of the others and said, "The wound is mortal. He won't survive it."

"Where's his wife?" Clint asked.

"I don't know," Leale said. "I suppose they took her to safety."

Clint turned and found himself looking at a soldier not much older than he was.

"We better clear the stairs and the front," Clint said. "Make a path in case they bring Mrs. Lincoln here."

The soldier, a corporal, said, "You're right. Come on."

Clint stopped by his room quickly for a shirt. Frieda, seeing him approach the door, handed him his shirt and his boots without opening the door more than she had to.

Clint pulled on the boots, donned the shirt, and then went to help the soldiers clear a path.

The vigil went on through the night. They did, indeed, bring Mrs. Lincoln to her husband's bedside, but the doctors soon exiled her to the front room, where she sat and sobbed.

She was soon joined by her sons, Robert and Tad. The secretary of the navy, Gideon Welles, soon arrived, followed by the secretary of war, Edwin M. Stanton.

It was Stanton who took over—in the absence of Vice President Andrew Johnson—running the government from the rear parlor of the house. He sent and received telegrams, and coordinated the search for John Wilkes Booth, who had been identified as the assassin. The vice president had been taken somewhere safe.

As the sun came up, Allan Pinkerton arrived—in his "E. J. Allan" persona—and was surprised to see Clint Adams there.

"How did you—"

"I have a room here."

Pinkerton nodded, said, "Don't leave," and was shown into Edwin Stanton's temporary command post.

At 7:22 a.m. Abraham Lincoln was pronounced dead. He was fifty-six years of age. His wife, Mary, was taken into his room. Clint managed to get in there, as well, along with the doctors, Secretary Welles, Secretary Stanton, and "E. J. Allan." The group knelt in the presence of the President's body, said a prayer, and then Edwin Stanton announced for all to hear, "Now he belongs to the ages."

# SIXTEEN

Secretary Stanton had the house cleared after Lincoln's death. At Pinkerton's behest, Clint was asked to stay. During all the commotion, Frieda had managed to slip out the back door. Clint didn't know if he'd ever see her again. In fact, he very much doubted it.

Clint sat in the front room, totally dressed and wearing his gun. Pinkerton was in the rear room with Secretary of War Stanton. Secretary Welles had left. The President's body had not yet been removed, but the Lincoln family had been transported back to the White House.

When Pinkerton came out of the back, too, Clint stood up.

"I want you in on this search," he said.

"Is it true it was John Wilkes Booth?" Clint asked Mr. "E. J. Allan."

"Yes. The bastard made no attempt to hide his identity. From witnesses' statements, we are fairly certain he injured himself when he jumped from the box to the stage."

"Why didn't someone on stage grab him?"

"Because they're actors," Pinkerton said, "and he was armed."

"Who's in on the search?"

"There are twelve soldiers who have been charged with the search to this point. Others are being deployed around the city and the outskirts of the city, but basically twelve men are trying to track him. I've got a buggy outside that will take you to them so you can join the search."

"What do you want me to do?"

"I want you to catch the bastard and bring him back," Pinkerton said.

"Allan, I'll bring him back, but alive. I'm not an assassin, no matter what he's done."

"You do what you have to do," Pinkerton said. "There'll be no questions asked."

"Did you hear me—"

"I understand your moral position, Adams!" Pinkerton said. "Now you understand mine. This son of a bitch has murdered an American hero, possibly one of the greatest presidents this country has ever had—and the goddamned war is over! There is no way to justify this act. You do whatever you think you have to do to bring him back, understand? In whatever condition. And he must have had accomplices. I want them all."

"Was this an isolated act?"

"Apparently not. At ten p.m. last night someone broke into Secretary of State Seward's house and tried to kill him while he was bedridden."

"They didn't succeed?"

"No, he was injured, stabbed, but he is not dead. They managed to drive the assassin away. Vice President Johnson and his family have been taken to the White House. Mr.

Lincoln's family also. They can all be protected there. But by God, before this night is over I'll know who else was in on this! Now go. Your transport is outside."

Clint joined the soldiers hunting for Booth, but by that evening he was back in Washington, meeting with Pinkerton in his office.

"The trail went cold," he told Pinkerton. "Somebody's hiding them."

"Damn it, man!" Pinkerton slammed his fist down on the desk. "I want Booth! And everyone who worked with him."

"You'll have them," Clint said, "but probably not today, or tomorrow. There has to be an investigation, Allan. You'll have to find out who his friends were, his co-conspirators, and he'll have to be found. Check all the doctors in and outside of the city. He can't have gotten that far."

"We found out that he stole a horse from outside the theater and rode off. He was most definitely not afoot. And he probably met up with whoever tried to kill Secretary Seward. From what we can tell, both attacks took place around ten o'clock. This was a coordinated effort. Well planned and—the Lincoln part, anyway—well carried out."

"I need some sleep, and a bath, and then I'll be ready to go."

"You have been discharged from my service," Pinkerton said. "You are not honor bound to continue to take part in this hunt."

"I would have no honor if I did not continue," Clint said.

"Very well," Pinkerton said, "but get as much sleep as you can now, for after today nobody sleeps until John

Wilkes Booth has been brought to justice. Do you understand that?"

"I understand it very well, sir," Clint said. "I'm in this
until the end."

# SEVENTEEN

The end came on April 26, twelve days after the shooting of Abraham Lincoln.

Clint had been working with a group of twelve soldiers—the same twelve who had been together from the beginning. They were acting on information received anonymously, that John Wilkes Booth and another conspirator named Herold, had been treated by a Maryland doctor named Dr. Mudd. After Mudd had set Booth's broken leg, he had taken them to the home of a Samuel Cox. After being at the Cox home for only a day, they moved on to a man named Thomas Jones, who hid them in a swamp very close to his house, until they could cross the Potomac River.

They remained at large until they found themselves in a barn on a farm owned by a man named Richard Garrett.

Acting on that information, Clint and the soldiers had tracked Booth and Herold to Garrett's farm, and trapped them in the barn.

After a few hours Herold came out and surrendered himself, but Booth refused to give himself up.

"So what do we do?" a private asked the lieutenant in charge. "Burn him out?"

"I don't think Mr. Garrett would appreciate having his barn burned down, soldier," Clint said. "Especially when it's not necessary. After all, where can Booth go?"

"He deserves to burn," another soldier said.

"Adams is right," the lieutenant said. "There's no need to destroy the man's property. We can afford to wait Booth out."

Some of the men grumbled.

"Corbett," the lieutenant said, "take Wilson and get close to the barn. See if you can see anything."

"Yes, sir," Corporal Boston Corbett said.

Corbett and Wilson slipped away into the darkness.

They could see light from inside the barn, shining out between some of the slats. Herold told them Booth was well armed, and had a storm lamp.

The lieutenant moved away from his men with Clint. He and Clint were roughly the same age, with the other men in the group being younger still. There had been an older sergeant with them in the beginning, but he had been reassigned for some reason. So the lieutenant pretty much had been depending on Clint for advice.

"What do you think?" he asked.

"I think we need to do something before these men of yours get lynch-mob fever."

"I think you're right."

"I suppose I could get close to the barn, see if there's a way in from the back. Then maybe—"

They were interrupted by a shot. All the men came to attention and looked toward the barn.

"He got 'im! He got 'im!" Wilson was shouting, as he ran back to the rest of the troop.

"What are you talking about, man?" the lieutenant demanded.

"Corbett got Booth!" Wilson said. "We was able to look into the barn through some loose slats. Corbett just pushed the barrel of his gun between 'em and took a shot—and he got 'im."

"Are you sure?" Clint asked.

"Booth is down," Wilson said. "We saw him go down."

The lieutenant and Clint exchanged a look, but before they could say anything, the other soldiers started running for the barn. Clint and the lieutenant followed. By the time they caught up, the men had broken down the barn door and were standing around the fallen figure of John Wilkes Booth. Boston Corbett was also standing there.

"What happened, man?" the lieutenant demanded.

Corbett had been looking down at Booth. Now he raised his head and looked at the lieutenant.

"I had the shot," he said, calmly, "so I took it."

Clint looked down at Booth. The shot had taken him in the neck, and from the look of him he was completely paralyzed.

"Let's get him outside—" the lieutenant started, but before he could even finish, two soldiers grabbed Booth's feet and dragged him out onto the steps of the barn.

"Take it easy!" Clint shouted.

"Easy?" one of the soldiers snapped. "With this Southern scum?"

"Hey, he's tryin' ta say somethin'," one of the other soldiers said.

The man leaned down close to Booth, but Clint was able to hear what Booth was saying.

"He's askin' for water," the soldier said.

"Let him die dry," one of the men said.

"Lieutenant?" asked the soldier who had leaned over Booth. His name was Robbins.

"Go ahead, if you want to."

Robbins opened his canteen. Booth was not able to raise his head, so the soldier just spilled some water into his mouth.

Booth looked at the soldier and said weakly, "Tell my mother I died for my country."

"Why that—" one of the other soldiers said, but he was restrained from rushing the dying man.

"What should we do with Booth, Lieutenant?" another man asked.

The lieutenant looked at Clint.

"He isn't going to last long," Clint said.

"Wilson," the lieutenant said, "go get the farmer. We'll want to borrow a team and wagon from him."

"Yes, sir."

Wilson ran off to the farmhouse.

"Whether he lasts or not, we'll take him back in the wagon," the lieutenant said.

"Hey, Boston," someone shouted, "you're a hero!"

Corporal Boston Corbett seemed unconcerned with the statement.

Two hours later, arrangements for the farmer's wagon still had not been made. Apparently, the man was bartering for it.

Booth looked as if he wanted to say something. Robbins once again leaned down to him, and once again Clint was able to hear.

He asked Robbins to lift his paralyzed arms for him.

"Useless . . . useless . . ." John Wilkes Booth said, and died.

# EIGHTEEN

"That's quite a story," Sheriff McKay said. "How did he get dubbed 'Lincoln's Avenger'?"

"I'm not sure," Clint said. "Might have been a newspaper story."

"You didn't say that you knew Corbett that well. I mean, that you were there when it happened."

"I didn't know him all that well," Clint said. "And, in fact, I wasn't right there when he fired. Only he was. No one saw him fire the shot."

"Was there ever any question that he fired it?" McKay asked.

"No," Clint said, "he obviously fired it."

"So how did he end up in an asylum so many years later?" McKay wondered.

"It's just the way his life went, I suppose," Clint said. "Initially declared a hero, he was also arrested and charged with disobeying orders, taking it on himself to shoot Booth.

The secretary of war stepped in and said Corbett was still a hero. There was also a reward, of which Corbett received about sixteen hundred dollars. When he was asked why he shot Booth, he said 'Providence directed me.' So rather than being arrested, he was discharged. I lost track of him then, until about eight or ten years ago."

"What happened then?"

"I ran into him," Clint said. "He was living in a dugout cave outside of Concordia, Kansas . . ."

## CONCORDIA, KANSAS, 1878

When Clint rode into Concordia, the incidents of Abraham Lincoln's death and what followed were a distant memory. He had not thought of Boston Corbett in many years.

He was in Concordia for a poker game. The buy-in was steep, but he was going to be facing some of the best players in the country, maybe the world, and he was looking forward to it. He was told that his friends Bat Masterson and Luke Short—the two best poker players of his acquaintance— were not able to attend, so as far as he knew he would be facing no friends at the table, which suited him.

It was, in fact, Bat Masterson who had recommended him for inclusion in the game, since he was not able to attend himself. Clint was not known for his poker playing, so having someone like Bat vouch for him was important. Clint had held his own in games against Bat and Luke many times, although he admitted they were better than him, simply because they played more than he did. They were, after all, gamblers. His reputation was as a gunman. Still, men like Bat Masterson and Ben Thompson were equally good at being both.

Clint reined in his horse in front of the Concordia House Hotel. Because he was a player in the game, a room had been arranged for him. It was all included in the buy-in—the room, his food, everything. He had even received word that women would be supplied—although he usually preferred to find his own women.

He dismounted and went inside. At the front desk he gave the clerk his name.

"Ah, yes, Mr. Adams," the fussy little man said. "We've been expecting you. Just sign here, please."

It wasn't the regular hotel register the man presented to him, but another, smaller book. The page he was signing was blank.

"Why not the register?" Clint asked.

"Well, you're here for the game, right?"

"Yes."

"The players sign in this book."

"Am I the first to arrive?"

"Oh, no, several players have arrived."

"But this page is blank."

"Each player gets his own page."

"Why is that?"

"Well, I assume it's so the players don't know about each other until they come to the table."

Clint shrugged, signed his name, and pushed the book back toward the clerk. It didn't really matter to him who the players were. He was looking forward to sitting down in a private game where all anyone wanted from him was his money, not his life.

"Room eleven, sir," the clerk said. "Top of the stairs and to the right. I hope you enjoy your stay. Our dining room is available to you, free of charge."

Clint turned and saw that the dining room was open.

"Can I have someone take care of your horse for you?" the man asked.

Clint was still riding his big black gelding, Duke, back then.

"No," Clint said, "I better do that myself. I don't want anybody to lose any fingers."

"Very well. The livery stable down the street will take care of your animal at no cost to you."

"Thanks. I'll take care of that, stow my gear in my room, and then go to the dining room—if anyone's looking for me."

"Yes, sir."

"Uh, do you know who the host of the game is?"

"Yes, sir, I do."

When the clerk said nothing more, Clint asked, "When do I find out?"

"You'll be notified as to where the game is tonight," the clerk said. "Don't worry, sir. They won't start without you."

"That's comforting," Clint said. "Thanks."

He left to see to Duke's comfort.

# NINETEEN

Clint gave Duke over to a suitably impressed livery man, left his saddlebags and rifle in his room, and went to the dining room for a steak. When it came, it was thick and red and cooked to perfection.

"Wow," the man at the next table said. He had stood up and was leaving money on his table to cover his bill. "Who do you know in the kitchen?"

"What do you mean?"

"Well, my steak was okay, but it didn't look anything like that," the man said.

The man left. Clint cut off a chunk of meat and tasted it. Ambrosia. The onions, potatoes, and vegetables were perfect, too. He did know somebody in the kitchen, he just didn't know who it was, yet.

After supper he went to the clerk and asked about a bath.

"Now, sir?"

"No, in the morning."

"What time?"

"Eight a.m.?"

"It'll be waiting for you, Mr. Adams."

"Thank you."

Clint went to his room with intentions of reading the Mark Twain book he'd recently picked up, the nonfiction *Old Times on the Mississippi*. After a few pages, the day of riding caught up to him, and he fell asleep.

In the morning he rose and found that a note had been slipped beneath his door. He took it out of the envelope and read it. It told him to be at the Concordia Cattleman's Club at eight p.m. that night. Nothing further. Apparently that was where the game was going to take place.

He went downstairs and had his bath. Then, feeling refreshed, he went to the dining room for a steak-and-eggs breakfast the likes of which he'd never had before. The meat was tender, the eggs perfect. He saw other people looking at his plate as they went by. He decided that by looking at people's breakfasts, he might be able to tell who some of the other players were.

He saw two other people with breakfasts that looked perfect, like his. A man and a woman, sitting separately. He decided not to approach them. He didn't want to make friends with any of the other players.

He paid his check and left the hotel.

He spent the day walking around Concordia. He could see this was a town that was growing by leaps and bounds. There were a lot of new buildings among the older ones, both brick and wood. It seemed as if each street had at least one saloon and one restaurant and, in between, many shops—hardware, feed and grain, leather goods, ladies' hats and clothing, a gun shop in which he spent some time, a shop selling men's hats, an ice cream emporium.

Check Out Receipt

Turner Park

Wednesday, June 29, 2022 5:49:12
PM

Item: 32022211027525
Title: Interlibrary loan material.
Due: 07/20/2022

Total items: 1

www.hpl.ca
Dial 905-546-3425 for account
information.

Thank you for visiting the Hamilton
Public Library.

He had lunch somewhere away from the hotel. He didn't want one of those perfect meals again from the hotel dining room. He stopped in a small café instead and had a satisfactory meal. Nobody gave his food a second look, and no one in the place seemed to be better fed than anyone else.

After that he left and stopped in one of the many saloons for a beer. He spent a lot of time over it, listening to the other patrons discuss town business. Again, no one gave him a second look. Clint usually tried to keep a low profile when he came to a new town.

Unfortunately, that wasn't always possible.

Clint was still killing time over a beer when the batwings opened and a man wearing a badge came in. There were only a few men in the saloon at that time of the afternoon, and his eyes immediately fell on Clint, who was not surprised.

The lawman walked over and Clint turned to face him.

"Afternoon, Sheriff," he said.

"Adams," the man said. "I heard you were comin' to town to play in the poker game."

"I figured you would," Clint said.

"My name's Reynolds, Sheriff Paul Reynolds," the man said. "Been sheriff here about four years. The town is growing. I have a couple of deputies and we keep it pretty quiet, except for some Friday and Saturday nights."

"That figures."

"I hope you're truly here to play poker, and that you won't be lookin' for trouble."

"I never look for trouble, Sheriff."

"But I'll bet it finds you, more times than not," the man said.

"Well, I can't argue with you there, but I really am here to play poker, so—"

He was cut off when the batwings opened violently and a deputy came running in.

"Sheriff, there's trouble."

"Where?"

"Outside of town," the man said. "You know, that dug-out where that crazy man lives?"

The sheriff looked at Clint.

"We got a nut livin' in a cave in a cliff wall outside of town," he said. "What's the problem, Jerry?"

"There's some boys were sayin' they're gonna go out there and get a look in that cave."

"We know the fella in the cave's got a gun," the sheriff said to Clint.

"Then why don't folks just leave him alone?" Clint asked. "That's probably why he lives in a cave."

"Some folks just can't leave other folks alone," the sheriff said. "I gotta go. I hope we don't have to talk again."

"Only if you sit down at the table across from me," Clint said.

"Not likely me gettin' into that game on my pay," the lawman said.

"Well then, good luck with your crazy man."

"Let's go, Jerry."

The two lawmen rushed out.

Clint finished his beer and also left. He decided to go back to his room and stay until he got hungry, spend his time with Mr. Twain. Then he'd have supper before the poker game started.

# TWENTY

Clint presented himself at the Cattleman's Club after another excellent steak at the Concordia House Hotel dining room.

A black man wearing white gloves greeted him at the door.

"Suh?"

Clint presented the note that had been slipped under his door.

"Yes, suh," the man said. "Follow me, please."

The black man led Clint through the club, which was crowded with well-dressed cattlemen and their guests, along with some not so well-dressed cattlemen and their guests. Clint figured he was somewhere between well dressed and not so well.

Down a long hallway to the rear of the building, they eventually reached a pair of double redwood doors. The black man turned both doorknobs and opened the door. Inside was a plushly furnished room dominated by a green felt-topped poker table that had seating for eight people. If they had a full table, they'd have to play five-card stud all night, not Clint's favorite game.

"Am I the first to arrive?" Clint asked.

"Yessuh," the black man said. "Mr. Baron will be in presently."

"Mr. Baron? Is that my host?"

"Yessuh."

"Is that his real name?"

"As far as I knows, suh. Excuse me."

The black man left and closed the door behind him. Clint walked to the poker table. In front of each player's chair, there was a cutout filled with different colored chips. Since he knew the amount of the buy-in, Clint was able to figure out the denominations of the chips. He was touching the green felt when the doors opened again and a tall, broad-shouldered man entered wearing a black suit. He had black hair that was slick with pomade, with some gray hair at the temples and in his mustache. Clint guessed him at fifty, but in very good shape.

"Mr. Adams," the man said. "I'm sorry to keep you waiting. I'm Mike Baron."

"Mr. Baron."

The two men shook hands.

"I'm going to presume to call you Clint, so you should call me Mike."

"All right, Mike."

"What do you think of the setup?"

"Very impressive."

"How about this?"

Baron walked to a blank wall, touched something, and the wall slid aside, revealing a fully stocked bar.

"We'll have a girl behind the bar at all times," he said.

"That's fine," Clint said, "but I don't drink while I'm playing."

"Really? I know a lot of people who can't play until they're properly loosened up."

"Well, I guess I play tighter than most people."

"Well, how about a drink now?"

"Beer?"

"Comin' up."

Baron got behind the bar, moved to the sole beer stick, and drew Clint a mug.

"There you go."

Clint approached the bar and accepted the mug. It was very cold.

"Thank you."

Baron poured himself something that looked like brandy.

"When I got that telegram from Bat Masterson recommending you for this game, I was very happy," Baron said.

"Glad to hear it."

"It shakes up the game, you know?" Baron said. "Somebody new, somebody unusual, somebody not known for playin' poker. It's gonna be real interestin'. How's your hotel room?"

"It's fine."

"And the food?"

"The food's great," Clint said. "Must be costing you a fortune to house and feed all the players."

"We have seven players," Baron said, pointing to the table. "The eighth slot is for the house dealer. It's really not that expensive. The hotel is sort of a sponsor for the game. Believe me, everybody makes out."

"Except the six players who don't win."

"Well," Baron said, "it is a winner-take-all game, after all."

At that moment the doors opened again, and the same black man entered, leading two other people.

"Ah, now the players are arriving," Baron said. "Let me introduce you."

# TWENTY-ONE

The six other players arrived at intervals of a minute or two, so within ten minutes all seven were seated at the table, along with the house dealer, who was introduced simply as Dexter.

Starting at Dexter's left the players were:

Zack Foxx, a gambler Clint had heard a story or two about. He was in his thirties and, according to Bat Masterson, adept at poker, but not in the class of a Luke Short.

Cole Weston, a gambler Clint knew nothing about, which seemed odd, because the man was in his sixties. He was white-haired and obviously given to wearing vividly colored vests.

Henry Mitchum, another gambler, but unlike Foxx and Weston, he was not wearing a suit, but trail clothes, albeit clean ones. He was in his mid-thirties, had a well-cared-for gun on his hip.

Pete Leslie, the youngest man in the room. He appeared to be in his late twenties, was wearing a gray suit rather than a black one, and seemed uncomfortable in it.

And the fifth man, the oddest of the bunch, Edgar Box, a fortyish, fussy little man with wire-framed glasses and all the mannerisms of a bank teller.

Clint was seated directly to Dexter's right.

"Gentlemen," Mike Baron said, "welcome to the Concordia Cattleman's Club Poker Game. I'm your host, Mike Baron. You're all here for a reason—you can play poker."

"And we paid the buy-in," Cole Weston said.

The other men laughed, except for Box. He was looking around the table, as if memorizing the faces of all his opponents.

"Your positions at the table were chosen at random, so please don't read anything into them," Baron said. "You are each beginning with ten thousand in chips. There is no re-buy. Once you lose, you're out. There will be a five-minute break every hour, a fifteen-minute break every three hours. You may each request one half-hour break at any time during the game. We will be playing dealer's choice. Each of you in turn will choose a game for Dexter to deal. Mr. Foxx, you will start. Good luck, gents."

"Mr. Foxx?" Dexter asked.

"Seven stud," Foxx said.

Dexter shuffled, Clint cut, and the game began.

After the first hour they broke for the first five-minute period. Clint was ahead. Peter Leslie was behind, half his money gone. Edgar Box still had most of his chips, because he had played very few hands. All the players but Clint and Box went to the bar for a drink.

"No drink for you, Mr. Adams?" Box asked. He had a very high, reedy voice.

"I don't drink while I play."

"Nor do I," Box said. "I believe this will give us an advantage."

"Only if we play well."

"Oh," Box said, "I don't believe that will be a problem . . . on my part."

"You sound very . . . confident." Actually, Clint thought Box sounded arrogant, and so far all the little man had done was watch.

Laughter came from the bar as the other players either made friends and bonded, or pretended to.

"Gentlemen," Baron announced, "back to the table, please."

Dexter had left the room, and now he reentered, as if on cue, and sat down, ready to deal.

"The deal is to Mr. Adams," Dexter said.

"Five-card draw," Clint said, "Jacks or better to open."

"Yes, sir."

Dexter dealt the cards out. Clint waited for all five cards to hit the table before he gathered them in and picked them up. Two players—Leslie and Weston—picked their cards up one at a time as they slid across the table to them. To Clint this exhibited a lack of patience. He felt patience, more than anything, would work in his favor.

He made a pair of kings. But before the play came to him, Cole Weston opened. Mitchum called, Leslie folded, Box called, Clint called, and Foxx folded.

There were four players left.

Weston took three cards.

Mitchum asked for one.

Box called for two cards.

Clint took two.

Clint figured Weston had opened with a pair, and only

aces could beat his kings. Mitchum couldn't open, but he called and asked for one card, so he was going for a straight or a flush. Box's call for two cards represented the first hand he had really played, and he was representing that he had three of a kind, because only an amateur would hold a kicker to a pair.

"Mr. Weston, you opened."

"Bet five hundred."

Mitchum folded in disgust. No straight, no flush.

Box called the five hundred and said, "Raise a thousand."

Clint might have believed one of them had he not drawn a third king. He couldn't fold this hand. Mitchum would have had to have opened with aces and then drawn another to beat him, and Box's three of a kind would then not be good. Of course, either man could have made a full house. If that was the case, they would deserve the hand.

"Call the fifteen hundred and raise the same."

"Twenty-five hundred to you, Mr. Mitchum," Dexter said.

Mitchum studied Clint's face, then said, "Fold," and dropped his cards on the table, facedown.

"Mr. Box?"

Box frowned, and his lips moved silently as if he was counting something.

"Raise two thousand," he said, finally.

"I call."

"Mr. Box, you've been called," Dexter said.

Box frowned, turned his cards over.

"Pair of aces."

Clint laid his cards out.

"Three kings," Dexter said, "the winner."

Box shook his head. Clint couldn't believe it. The little

man had been dealt aces and had kept a kicker to try to convince the table he had been dealt three of a kind. The first play he made all night and it was a foolish one like that.

Clint was tempted to disregard him as a threat, but the fact of the matter was, the man might have been sandbagging them all, trying to look foolish.

"That wasn't very smart," Leslie said.

Box said nothing.

"Looks like he kept a kicker," Leslie said.

"Could you analyze my play quietly, sir?" Edgar Box asked.

"Can't I talk?" Leslie asked. He looked at the dealer. "Hey, Dex, we allowed to talk?"

"There is no rule against it," Dexter said. "Mr. Foxx, the deal is yours."

"Five-card stud," Foxx said. So far everyone had played seven-card stud or draw. "Let's just shake it up a bit."

# TWENTY-TWO

"Anybody hear about that guy who lives in a cave outside of town?" Leslie asked.

"I heard somethin' about that," Weston said. "What's the story?"

"I'm not sure," Leslie said. "I heard some boys went out there to hoorah a guy who lives in a cave—a dugout, really. Heard the sheriff and his deputy had to go out and stop it before it got started."

"What's a fella doin' livin' in a cave?" Mitchum asked.

"Don't know," Leslie said. "I was kinda hopin' one of you knew somethin'. Dex? You live here. You know anythin' about it?"

Dexter shrugged. He was about thirty, and dealt like a man who was born with a deck of cards in his hands. Clint watched him very closely to see if he was trick dealing at all, but if he was, he was doing it very well.

"All I know is he showed up about three weeks ago, bought some supplies, said somethin' about livin' in a cave outside of town. Folks started gettin' curious about him."

"Anybody find out his name?" Foxx asked.

"I'm sure somebody knows it," Dexter said, "but I don't. Mr. Weston, you bet."

They finished the hand and then Dexter finished what he was saying.

"All I know is somebody said he was called 'Lincoln's Avenger.'"

"What?" Clint asked.

Dexter looked at him.

"Lincoln's Avenger," the dealer said, again.

"Who calls him that?" Clint asked. "Does he call himself that?"

"I don't know," Dexter said. "I don't know who calls him that. I just know somebody said it. Why?"

"I heard of somebody called that," Clint said, "that's all. Wonder if it's the same guy."

"What did your guy do to get called that?" Peter Leslie asked.

Clint hesitated, then said, "He shot John Wilkes Booth."

"He what?" Weston asked.

"Shot Booth," Clint said, "after Booth shot Abe Lincoln."

"Yer kiddin'," Weston said.

"No, I'm not."

"That can't be this fella," Dexter said.

"Why not?"

"This man's a nut, not a hero."

"How do you know that?"

"I don't know it, not for sure," Dexter said, "but . . ."

"Anybody can be a hero," Clint said.

"That would depend on which side you fought on," Box said.

Zack Foxx asked, "Were you a Southerner, Mr. Box?"

"I did not fight in the war, sir," Box said, "but I am from the South, yes."

"So you don't think the man who shot Booth was a hero?" Weston demanded. "You think Booth was a hero for shooting Lincoln?"

"Booth was a patriot," Box said. "He was also a fool."

"A patriot and a fool?" Leslie asked. "That's some combination."

"A patriot because he thought he was doing something for his country," Box said, "and a fool because he got caught."

"Boy," Weston said, "I ain't sure I like you."

"Me, neither," Foxx said.

"I'm sure I don't care whether you like me or not, gentlemen," Box said. "I'm here to take your money, regardless."

"Yeah, well," Foxx said, "not by holdin' a kicker to a pair of aces."

Clint saw a small smile form on Edgar Box's face.

"The war's been over for years, boys," Clint said. "Let's play poker."

# TWENTY-THREE

During the first fifteen-minute break Clint went to the bar. Mike Baron came into the room for each break, even though he had a pretty girl tending bar for the players.

Clint called Baron over to the side.

"What do you know about this fellow who lives in a cave outside of town?"

"Not much, why?"

"It came up during the game," Clint said. "It sounded like he might be somebody I once knew."

"Really? As far as I know he's a hermit, or a nut, or both. Would you like me to ask around, maybe find out his name?"

"I'd appreciate it."

"Sure, no problem, Clint," Baron said. "How's the game goin'?"

"It's going."

"I heard Box held a kicker to a pair of aces. I hate to think I let somebody like that into the game."

"You never know about some people's tactics," Clint said.

"You mean . . . you think he did it on purpose?" Baron asked.

Clint shrugged.

"Ask your dealer to analyze the game for you," Clint said.

"I understand," Baron said. "You don't want anything getting back to the other players."

"Everybody analyzes the game in his own way," Clint explained.

"I understand," Baron said. "I'll try to get that information for you."

"I'd be obliged," Clint said.

He went back to the table, where Box sat, playing with his chips, his lips moving. The others were at the bar, flirting with the bartender, or crying into their drink, if they were Peter Leslie. He was down to his last thousand.

Clint was still ahead, Box was ahead, and it looked like Zack Foxx was ahead. The others were losing.

"You didn't have to do what you did, you know," Box said.

"What's that?"

"Come to my defense."

"I thought I was trying to get the game back on track."

"Nevertheless," Box said, "I can handle myself."

"I'm starting to see that," Clint said.

"What does that mean?"

"That bit about keeping a kicker," Clint said. "That was a good trick."

"Meaning what?"

"You didn't have to show your hand," Clint said. "You could have laid it down, facedown. You wanted everyone to see what you'd done, so they'd think you were a bad player."

"Is that right?"

"Yeah, Edgar," Clint said. "That's right. I don't know how many of the other players have it figured right, but I do."

"You are a gunman," Box said. "What do you know about good poker?"

Clint laughed and said, "I guess that's what we're going to find out."

# TWENTY-FOUR

Pete Leslie was the first to bust out of the game, followed soon by Zack Foxx. The two men did not leave the room, though. As the sun streamed through the windows, they were standing at the bar, still drinking, still talking to the pretty bartender—who, Clint was sure, was the third bartender of the night. Both men were armed, and both had seemed to be watching Edgar Box all night. Clint knew that many men from both the North and the South were still fighting the Civil War. He figured to keep an eye on both men. He didn't want them killing Edgar Box before Clint took all the man's money.

"You're friends with Bat Masterson, aren't you?" Box asked him.

Clint looked at the little man.

"You've done very little talking tonight, Edgar," he said, "and now you want to know about my friends?"

From the way the chip stacks looked, Clint and Edgar were well ahead of the others. Cole Weston seemed to be maintaining his buy-in, while the other player, Mitchum, was hanging on by a thread.

"Just trying to make some conversation," Box said.

"That hasn't been part of your game up to now," Clint said. "Why change? You look like you're doing pretty good."

"He's lucky," Mitchum said, "that's all. Just dumb luck."

"I wouldn't be callin' somebody else dumb, if I were you, Mr. Mitchum," Box said.

It seemed to Clint that Box had suddenly decided to start talking, start antagonizing some of the other players. It had worked with Foxx. It might have worked with Leslie, but he was out of the game by the time Box started his new tactic.

And it was working with Mitchum, who was getting all riled up. In an effort to show Box up, he called the little man's next raise and busted out of the game.

That left Clint, Box, and Cole Weston. Box's tactic wasn't going to work on Clint or Weston, so he fell silent once it was just the three of them.

They broke for fifteen minutes at that point, and Clint pulled Mike Baron to one side.

"What is it?"

"I don't think you should let Leslie, Foxx, and Mitchum stay in the room and watch. They're drinking and getting all worked up about the Civil War."

"Why is that a problem?"

"Edgar Box is obviously a Southerner," Clint said. "He's been using that to stir them up."

"Dexter's from the South, too," Baron said. "Is he gettin' worked up?"

"No," Clint said, "he hasn't even mentioned it."

"What's your worry, Clint?"

"I think they might get worked up enough to try something."

"Like what?"

"You're being naive, Mike," Clint said. "I think they might try to kill him."

Baron scratched his head.

"Well, the rule of the game has always been that eliminated players can stay and watch, but . . . Don't you think putting them out might rile them up even more?"

"It might," Clint said. "How about taking away their guns?"

"That's not somethin' I'd like to try to do," Baron said. "What about you?"

"I promised the sheriff I'd stay out of trouble," Clint said. "Trying to take another man's gun might cause some."

"Then you see where I'm stuck, Clint," Baron said.

Clint looked at the three men standing at the bar with their heads together. Weston was standing alone at the other end. Edgar Box, as always, remained seated. He'd gotten up one time, and that was for a glass of water.

"Maybe if you just kept an eye out, you could head off trouble if it looked like it was comin'."

"Okay," Clint said, "maybe I'll talk to Weston, see if he'd be willing to help."

"Okay," Baron said. "You've got five minutes left."

Clint walked to the other end of the bar and stood next to Weston.

"Anticipating trouble?" Weston asked.

"You see it, too?"

"Oh, yeah," Weston said. "Those three are just busting to put a bullet into that fussy little man. Hopefully, it won't be till after the game."

Weston was right. And the three would probably agree. They wouldn't try anything in that room. They'd wait until the game was over and then lie for Box outside.

"If anything happens," Clint said, "can I count on you?"

Weston sipped his drink.

"I'm sixty-three years old, Adams," Weston said. "I've always been ready to do what I have to to stay alive. That's what you can count on me for."

Clint was about to reply when he realized that might just be enough.

# TWENTY-FIVE

Over the next two hours Clint and Edgar Box systematically took all of Cole Weston's chips. When he busted out of the game, he did so with more charm than the other three put together.

"Good luck to you gents," he said, leaving the table.

"Gonna stay around and watch, Weston?" Foxx asked.

"Got no reason to do that," Weston said.

"Don't you wanna see who wins?" Leslie asked.

"I didn't win," the big man said. "That's all I care about. See you gents."

Before he left, he said to Dexter, "Nice dealing, kid."

"Thanks, Mr. Weston."

"If I had any money left, I'd tip you," he said, and left.

Dexter laughed and said, "Don't worry about it, Mr. Weston," to the dead air the man had left behind. "You gents want a break?"

One of the other rules of the game was a ten-minute break after elimination—if it was requested.

"I don't need a break," Clint said.

"Neither do I," Box said. "Deal the cards."

It came down, as it always did, to one last hand.

The game was seven-card stud. Both men had three cards to a flush on the table. In addition, the three cards were also to a straight—or, with a little luck, a straight flush.

"I call your last raise," Clint said. "All my money's in the pot."

"Mine, too," Box said.

"Two straight flushes would be some finish to this game," Zack Foxx said.

He and the other players had moved up to the table to watch. Mike Baron was there, also. There was one last card to come, the final down card.

Dexter dealt them out, set the deck down on the table, and settled back to watch.

"All the money is in the pot," he announced, "so there is nothing left to do but show."

Box was sweating.

"Look at Johnny Reb sweat," Mitchum said. "He was bluffin' and Adams got 'im."

Clint hoped that was true, because he had also been bluffing. He didn't have his flush, or his straight flush.

"Box?" Clint asked.

"You show."

"I call you."

Dexter said, "Mr. Adams is right. Mr. Box, you show first."

Box looked around, then smiled and showed his straight. Four red cards—diamonds—and a black one, a spade. The spade was a queen.

Clint showed his cards. He had a straight, also—four black cards—spades—and one red one, a king of hearts.

"There ya go," Foxx shouted. "One for the North."

"It's still just a poker game, Foxx," Clint said, "not a war."

"Adams," Baron said. "If you come with me, I'll cash you out."

"A pleasure," Clint said, standing. He looked at Box. "Wish I could say the same for playing with you, Edgar. You could use a lesson in manners."

"Yeah," Mitchum said, happily, "he already got a lesson in poker!"

Edgar Box stood up and quickly left the room. The others went to the bar for a last drink. Clint followed Mike Baron to his office.

"That was pretty good, Clint," Baron said. "I was convinced one of you was bluffin'."

"We both were, kind of," Clint said.

"How do you want your money?" Baron asked. "If you want cash, we'll have to go to the bank."

"I'll take a bank draft, Mike," Clint said, "and I'll put it into the bank myself."

"As you wish."

Baron sat down and wrote out a draft.

"That's for all of it, minus my cut."

Clint took the draft, looked at it.

"That's some cut."

"I had a lot of expenses."

"You told me putting the men up and feeding them was no expense. You said the hotel was a sponsor."

"Yes, but—"

Clint tore the bank draft up.

"I think you better refigure the amount, Mike," Clint said.

"Now wait—"

"Now!" Clint said.

Grumbling, Mike Baron wrote out a new bank draft with a revised number and handed it to Clint.

"That seems a little more like it," Clint said. "I have to say I question the quality of some of your players, and the way you operate, in general."

"This game has a big reputation," Baron said. "The quality's never been questioned, and neither have I."

"Then I guess your past winners were just happy to win and didn't realize what kind of cut you were taking," Clint said. "I won't be coming back here, Mike, and I'm sure the likes of Bat Masterson and Luke Short won't, either."

"You can't bad-mouth this game," Baron said. "You'll damage my credibility."

"Seems to me you're doing a good job of that on your own," Clint said. "See you, Mike."

Clint started for the door, leaving an unhappy Mike Baron seated at his desk. When Clint got to the door, though, he remembered something.

"By the way, what did you find out about that fella in the cave?"

"Huh? Oh, not much. I was you, I'd talk to the sheriff. He seems to know all about it."

"Okay, I'll do that," Clint said. He waved the bank draft. "Much obliged."

# TWENTY-SIX

Clint went to the Bank of Concordia and, because of the size of the bank draft, was asked to step in to see the president of the bank, Mr. John Harvey.

"This is quite a sizable sum, Mr. Adams," Harvey said, "quite a sizable sum."

"I'm sure it is, Mr. Harvey," Clint said, "but it can't be the largest you've ever seen."

"Oh, no, no," Harvey said. "I've been a bank manager or president for most of my forty banking years, Mr. Adams."

"Also," Clint said, "as you can see, the money won't even be leaving your bank."

Yet, he added to himself.

"Yes, I do see that," Harvey said. "Well, make yourself comfortable, sir. Just let me get a receipt for your deposit."

"I'll wait right here," Clint assured the man.

"Uh, yes, of course," Harvey said.

After he left the bank with his deposit receipt safely in his pocket, Clint walked to the sheriff's office. When he entered, Sheriff Reynolds was coming out from the cell block.

"Guests?" Clint asked.

"No, thank God," Reynolds said. "Just keepin' the accommodations clean. What can I do for you? I heard you won."

"That's on the street, already? Great."

"I hope you banked it."

"I did, but not everybody is going to realize that," Clint said.

Reynolds sat behind his desk.

"Not like you need any extra reasons for trouble to find you. Maybe you should leave town."

"That was very subtle, Sheriff," Clint said. "I'm impressed."

"I got some bad coffee here," the sheriff said, standing up. "You look like you ain't been to bed yet."

"I haven't, and I'll take any kind of coffee."

The sheriff poured out two cups, handed one to Clint, and went back to his desk. Clint sipped the cofee, and found it hot and to his liking.

"What's wrong with this?"

"Too strong."

"Coffee can't be too strong," Clint said.

"Have a seat, Mr. Adams, and tell me what's on your mind."

Clint sat and said, "The man who lives in the cave outside of town."

"What about him?"

"What's his name?"

"Why are you interested?"

"I heard something last night that makes me think I may know him," Clint said. "Is his name Boston Corbett?"

"To tell you the truth, I don't know his name," Sheriff Reynolds said. "I've only ever talked to him on two occasions."

"Was yesterday one of them?"

"No," the lawman said. "I rode out there and managed to talk some sense into about half a dozen boys who were feelin' their oats. Never did see the man in the cave."

"Well then," Clint said, "I guess I'll have to ride out there myself and find out."

"Be careful," Reynolds said. "He's got a rifle in there and he doesn't like visitors."

"I'll keep that in mind," Clint said.

"And if you have to kill 'im, please let me know about it."

"I'm not going to kill him, Sheriff," Clint said, "but since you brought that up . . ."

He told the sheriff about Edgar Box, how he had antagonized the other players at the table, and how Clint thought there might be trouble.

"The Civil War," Reynolds said, shaking his head. "Is that war ever gonna be truly over?"

"I don't even know if Box was truly a Southerner or not," Clint said. "He may have just been trying to throw these men off their game."

"Sounds like he did a good job of it."

"No," Clint said, "they just never had much game to begin with."

"I see. And you?"

"Me?" Clint asked, with a grin. "I just got lucky at the right time."

"Uh-huh," Reynolds said.

"Much obliged for the coffee."

"Sure thing. Any idea how much longer you'll be stayin'?"

"No," Clint said, "but when I find that out, I'll let you know. Um, can you give me directions to that cave?"

## TWENTY-SEVEN

# TWENTY-SEVEN

Clint followed the directions the sheriff gave him and spotted the cave right off. It wasn't particularly hidden, but it was certainly defensible by a man with one rifle.

Clint reined Duke in a good distance from the cave and decided to approach it on foot. He dropped the reins to the ground, knowing that the big gelding would not move unless he called him. He untied the burlap sack from the saddle horn.

As he walked toward the cave, Clint wondered if Boston Corbett would even remember him. They were never friends, and all they'd had in common was the hunt for John Wilkes Booth. Boston had killed Booth on his own, and had to withstand a possible court-martial before being dubbed "Lincoln's Avenger."

The powers that be at the time wanted Booth alive so they could question him, but in the end they figured they'd gotten everyone who was involved in the conspiracy to kill Lincoln.

Clint never knew what happened to Boston Corbett. He was always a loner, and Clint knew he'd left the service after a while and disappeared.

Clint was getting closer when the first shot came. The bullet hit the dirt well in front of him. He continued on. The second shot ricocheted off a rock to his left, closer to his foot.

"That's close enough!" a voice called out. "I don't like anybody comin' near me."

"Boston Corbett?" Clint shouted.

There was no reply, but there wasn't a shot, either, which Clint found encouraging.

"Boston Corbett?"

Silence.

Then: "Who're you?"

"My name's Clint Adams," Clint said. "If you're Boston Corbett, you'll probably remember my name."

More silence, and then, "You were there."

Clint knew what he meant.

"You were there, huntin' Booth."

"That's right."

"You were there, when I shot 'im," the man said. "You know."

"I didn't actually see you shoot him, Boston," Clint said, "but I know."

"Whataya want?"

"Well, for one thing I brought you some supplies. Not a lot, but a few things."

"And?"

"I just heard something in town that made me think you were here. I wanted to see how you were."

Silence.

For a moment Clint thought the man might just shoot at him again, but then he yelled, "Come ahead! I won't shoot ya."

Clint hoped that was a promise he could depend on the man to keep.

"Do you need any water? I can bring my canteen," Clint called out.

"I got water. Just come ahead."

Clint started toward the mouth of the cave.

When his deputy came in, Sheriff Reynolds said, "Jerry, Clint Adams went out to see that nut in the cave."

"What fer?" Jerry asked.

"He's got some idea that he knows the man," Reynolds said. "Claims he might be Boston . . . somebody. The man who shot John Wilkes Booth."

"Really? You mean we got us a celebrity in town? And a celebrity livin' in that cave?"

"Just be aware," Reynolds said. "I'm gonna go have lunch. If you hear about anything happenin', you let me know."

"Whataya think will happen?" Jerry asked, frowning.

"Oh, I don't know," the sheriff said, "maybe they'll end up killin' each other."

"Gawd," Jerry said, "that'd be awful."

"Yeah," Sheriff Reynolds said, "it'd be terrible."

Sheriff Reynolds stopped in to see Mike Baron before he went to lunch.

"I been lookin' for you," Baron said.

"What about?"

"That Adams, he robbed me."

"Did he? At gunpoint?"

"Well . . . no, but he had his hand on his gun."

"And took money from you?"

"No, he made me write him a bank draft."

"Wouldn't you do that anyway, Mike?" the sheriff asked. "I mean, he won, didn't he?"

"Yeah, but . . . he made me pay him more . . . more than—"

"I get it, Mike," Reynolds said. "He caught you tryin' to cheat him and made you pay him fair and square."

"Yeah, that's what I said," Baron replied. "He robbed me!"

# TWENTY-EIGHT

Clint reached the mouth of the cave. The man was still standing in the shadows as he entered. Once Clint was enveloped by the dark, he was able to see the man better.

"Boston Corbett," he said.

"You can tell?"

The man standing before him had a beard, long, straggly hair, dirty clothes, and was bigger and heavier than the Boston Corbett he had known some twelve or thirteen years before.

"Yes," Clint said. "Yes, I can tell."

"Come on," Corbett said, "I'll show you my home."

Clint followed Corbett down a long tunnel until they came out into a hollowed-out cavern. There was a fire going, which both lit the cave and kept it warm.

"Did you do this?" Clint asked. "I mean . . ."

"No, the cavern was here. I just sort of . . . hollowed it out some more. It's really pretty comfortable." He pointed to a bunch of rags. "There's my bed." He looked at the sack in Clint's hand. "Those my supplies?"

"Yes," Clint said, handing them over. "Some canned peaches, beans, coffee, and some beef jerky."

"Good," Corbett said. "Thanks."

"You, uh, do have something to cook those in, don't you?"

"I've got a pan, and a coffeepot. In fact, I have some coffee made. Want some?"

Clint hadn't smelled any coffee when he came in, so he assumed it was very weak.

"No, thanks."

"I don't blame you," Corbett said. "It's real weak. Hey, I tell ya what. I'll make a new pot with this stuff you bought me."

"Sure," Clint said. "That'd be good."

"Have a seat."

Clint sat by the fire and watched Corbett dump out the old, weak coffee and make a new pot. Instantly, the cavern was filled with the scent of strong coffee.

"Well," Corbett said, sitting across the fire from Clint. "I ain't smelled that in a while."

He scratched his neck, and seemed to catch something there and flick it away. Corbett could have used a bath or two.

Pretty soon each of them had a cup of coffee in his hands. Corbett offered Clint a piece of beef jerky, but Clint refused. He didn't want to eat any of the man's only food.

"Boston," Clint said, "I've got to ask. How did you come to be here?"

"You want me to go back over the past dozen years?" Corbett asked. "I don't want to. All I can tell you is, if I had the chance to shoot or not shoot John Wilkes Booth again, I wouldn't do it."

"Why did you?"

"I couldn't resist," Corbett said. "I had the shot. It was right there in front of me."

"But you had no orders to shoot."

"I know that," Corbett said. "Don't you think I think about that every day? I do. I told you, I wouldn't do it again. My life's been hell since I got called 'Lincoln's Avenger.'"

He bit into a piece of beef jerky and chewed vigorously.

"All I want is to be left alone."

"I understand there was some trouble out here yesterday," Clint said. "That's how I heard you were here."

"Just some yahoos who wanted to play games with the crazy hermit," Corbett said. "I was ready for them, but the sheriff got them to leave."

Clint sat back, finished his coffee, then got up.

"Why'd you come out here?" Corbett asked, also standing.

"I heard somebody say 'Lincoln's Avenger' was out here," Clint said. "I wanted to come and see for myself if it was really you."

"Well," Boston Corbett said, with a shrug, "it's me."

"Are you okay?" Clint asked.

"Actually," Corbett said, "I could be pretty happy here if folks would leave me alone. I can hunt and fish. There's even a lady from town who comes out and leaves baskets of food for me sometimes."

"Well, that's good," Clint said. "You need some clothes?"

"I could use a fresh shirt."

"I got an extra one in my saddlebags," Clint said. "I can give you that."

"I'd appreciate it."

They walked to the mouth of the cave together. As Clint stepped out, Corbett stopped.

"What's wrong?" Clint asked.

"I'll wait here while you go get it."

Clint turned to face the man.

"Boston, you don't trust me?"

"We haven't seen each other in a lot of years, Adams," Corbett said. "And we weren't great friends back then. But even if I trust you, somebody could have followed you out here."

He was right.

"I'll get the shirt."

From a point high above Clint and Boston Corbett, Edgar Box watched as Clint walked to his horse, took out a blue shirt, and carried it back to the cave. It was vivid blue. That was good. It would make a good target.

But not right now, Box thought.

Clint handed Corbett the shirt.

"Much obliged."

"I'm probably only going to be in town another day or so," Clint said, "but I'll try to bring you something else you need."

"I don't know what I need."

"Well," Clint said, "I'll just bring you something."

"Anything you bring would be appreciated."

The two men did not shake hands, and Clint left.

# TWENTY-NINE

Clint got back to Concordia, left Duke at the livery, and went for a beer. While he drank it, he wondered if he could ever live the way Boston Corbett was living. Probably not, but then he would probably never have reason to.

Or would he? What if his reputation—already formidable—continued to get bigger and bigger, until he had no peace. Would he then try to find a different sort of place to live, to be alone? And could that place ever end up being a hole in a cliff wall?

He was ordering a second beer when Sheriff Reynolds entered the saloon and joined him at the bar.

"Buy you one?" Clint asked.

"I guess that depends."

"On what?"

"On whether or not you'd be using the money you coerced out of Mike Baron."

Clint turned to face Reynolds.

"Coerced?"

"Actually, what he said was, you robbed him."

"I won his poker game," Clint said, "and when it comes time to pay me off, he claims I robbed him?"

Reynolds took some torn pieces of paper from his pocket and set them on the bar.

"This look familiar?"

"Looks like the bank draft I tore up in Baron's office."

"Why would you tear up a bank draft?" Reynolds asked. "I mean, I assume this was supposed to be your money?"

"That's right."

"Then why tear it up?"

"It wasn't enough."

"Why not?"

"Baron was taking too big a cut."

"Isn't that how he makes money?" the sheriff asked. "Host a big game, take a cut?"

"That's right."

"So you didn't like the cut he took?"

"That's right."

"So you made him pay you more?"

"I suggested to him that he pay me what I was owed," Clint said.

"How did you suggest it?"

"What do you mean?"

"I mean, did you point a gun at him when you were suggesting it?"

"I only draw my gun when I'm going to use it, Sheriff," Clint said, "so if I had drawn my gun, Baron would be dead."

"I see."

"Sheriff, Baron's just trying to get his money back. What I can't understand is why?"

"Me, either," the sheriff said. "Baron runs games all year. If he tried to cheat you, or claims you robbed him when you didn't, he's going to ruin his own reputation. Why would he do that?"

"Because I planned on ruining his reputation myself," Clint explained.

"Why would you do that?"

"Because he tried to cheat me," Clint said. "Should we go back to the beginning, Sheriff? I won, and when it came time to pay me off, he tried to cut too much and I called him on it."

"And you told him you were gong to tell people about it."

"Right."

"And were you?" the sheriff asked. "Or were you just tryin' to put a scare into him?"

"I was going to tell both Bat Masterson and Luke Short about it."

"Why them?"

"They both know Baron," Clint said. "Bat was the one who got me into the game."

"Why would he do that, if Baron's a crook?" Sheriff Reynolds asked.

"I don't know," Clint said, "but I'm going to ask him when I see him."

Reynolds picked up the pieces of the bank draft and put them back in his pocket.

"Adams, you're a stranger in Concordia, and Mike Baron is a respected member of our community."

"And what does that mean?"

"Who do you think I should believe?"

"Me."

"Why?"

"Because I'm telling the truth."

"Well," Reynolds said, "I'll have to be the judge of that. Don't leave town until I do decide."

"Would you come after me if I did?"

"I'd do my job, Adams," Reynolds said. "I know your reputation, but I would do my job."

He started for the door, then turned back.

"Don't go near Mike Baron until I sort this out," he said.

Clint raised his beer mug to the man.


"How can I help you, Mr. Adams?" John Harvey asked.

"My money," Clint said.

"What about it?"

"Is it still here?"

"Of course," Harvey said, "unless you took it out."

"I didn't."

"Then why would you ask?"

"Apparently, Mike Baron is claiming I coerced it out of him," Clint said. "He went to the sheriff. Would the sheriff be able to take that money out of the bank?"

"Not without a court order."

"So with a court order he could take the money out?" Clint asked.

"Or freeze the account so you can't get to it."

"I see. Well then, I would like to make a withdrawal, Mr. Harvey."

"You want to take the money out?"

"That's what I said."

"But you just said the sheriff—"

"Has the sheriff been here yet?"

"Well, no."

"No court order?"

"No."

"Then there's no reason I can't take the money out."

"No, there isn't . . . I suppose."

"Then I would like to do that . . . now!"

"Uh, of course," the bank manager said. "Just a moment." He stood up.

"I'll come with you."

"But why?"

"Because I don't want you stalling me and then sending for the sheriff."

"Why would I—"

"Yeah, yeah," Clint said. "Let's go and get my money, Mr. Harvey."

Clint left the bank with the money in his saddlebags. Twenty-five thousand dollars. Each man had bought into the game for five thousand. Baron had tried to take a third of it when a more likely cut would have been ten percent.

Now the question was where to put it to keep it safe when he couldn't even trust a bank.

# THIRTY

"I didn't expect you to come back so soon," Corbett said to Clint.

"I brought you some more supplies," Clint said. He held out two more sacks.

"Thank you."

"More canned goods, some salted pork, more jerky, coffee . . . even some peppermint sticks."

"Thank you," Corbett said. He set the bags aside, then looked across the fire at Clint. "What's in the saddlebags?"

"Twenty-five thousand dollars."

"That for me, too?"

"Not all of it."

"How much of it?"

"You tell me."

"How much money do I need living in a cave?"

"I don't know, Boston."

"So what do I have to do for this money?"

"Just hold onto it."

"Why?"

Clint explained.

"So you can't trust the bank and you think you can trust me?"

"I'm hoping I can."

"What makes you willing to take that chance?"

"I think you're an honorable man. I think that's what made you shoot Booth. I mean, it certainly wasn't a desire to be a hero."

"How long do you want me to hold it for?"

"Until I clear this whole thing up and am able to leave town."

Corbett nodded. "Okay."

He put his hand out over the fire.

Clint handed over the saddlebags.

"Boston—"

"You don't need to say it," Corbett said. "If I abscond with your money, you will track me down and kill me."

"Now all we need to do is agree on your fee for this favor."

"You don't take a fee for favors, Clint," Corbett said.

"Okay, then we need to decide how much of a donation I'll make to you."

"Well," Corbett said, "if it's a donation, it's your decision."

Corbett got up, walked into a darkened corner, and came back without the saddlebags.

"Don't worry," he said. "They'll still be here when you get back."

"I'm not worried," Clint said.

Much.

The door to the sheriff's office slammed open and Mike Baron stormed in.

"Adams has pulled a fast one!"

"What kind of fast one?" Sheriff Reynolds asked.

"I just heard from Harvey," Baron said. "He withdrew the money."

Reynolds grinned.

"He's smart. He knew we could freeze the account with a court order and he beat us to it."

"So now where is he?" Baron asked.

"That's what I need to find out," Reynolds said.


Clint rode back into town, hoping he'd made the right decision about Boston Corbett. But faced with the sheriff, the bank manager, and maybe a judge in town conspiring against him, what else was he to do?

When Clint entered the hotel, the clerk called him over.

"I'm sorry, uh, sir, but you'll have to, uh, settle your bill."

"My bill?"

"Yes, sir."

"But I'm not checking out."

"That's already been taken care of, sir."

"What do you mean?"

"You've already been, uh, checked out?"

"I see. My bill was supposed to be taken care of."

"I, uh, don't know anything about that, sir. I'm just a clerk."

"I see. Well, how much is my bill?"

The clerk pushed a piece of paper to Clint.

"Seems a little steep," he said.

"I, uh, think that includes the, uh, meals, sir."

"I see. Well, okay."

The clerk heaved a sigh of relief when Clint took out some money and paid his bill.

"Can you tell me who owns this hotel?"

"Uh, well, sir, I'm not supposed to—"

Clint peeled off another bill and held it out to the man.

"Uh, the hotel is owned by Mike Baron . . ."

"I see."

". . . and Sheriff Reynolds."

"They're partners?"

"Yes, sir," the clerk said, "and in more than just the hotel."

"I see."

"I—I can't say no more, Mr. Adams."

"That's okay," Clint said. "You've already said enough."

"There wasn't much of nothin' in your room, sir," the clerk said.

"No," Clint said, "I have everything with me. Good-bye."

Clint didn't bother to ask the clerk about other places to stay. In a town the size of Concordia there had to be some place that wouldn't be influenced by either Baron or Sheriff Reynolds.

# THIRTY-ONE

Clint found a boardinghouse run by a thirtyish widow who said all her rooms were empty.

"You can have your pick," she told him.

The house was old, but clean and well kept. It was also on a side street, but not completely off the beaten path.

"I've stayed in a lot of boardinghouses over the years," he told the woman. "It seems to me this one would be pretty popular."

"And my food is good," she said. "However, since I refuse to pay money to certain people—"

"Like the sheriff?"

"Then you've met the sheriff?"

"I have."

"Well, he and Mr. Baron own a lot of property in Concordia, and the property they don't own is paying protection money to them."

"Yes, I know Baron, too," Clint said. "Well, Mrs. Lacy, I'd be happy to stay here, if you'll have me."

"I'll be very happy for your company, Mr. Adams. Would you like something to eat?"

"I'd love something to eat."

"Well, go on upstairs, choose a room, and then come back down. I'll have something hot waiting for you."

"Thank you, Mrs. Lacy," he said.

"I think you can call me Olivia . . . Clint."

"All right, Olivia," he said. "I'll be right back."

He carried his rifle up to his room. He didn't have much else. He'd given his extra shirt to Boston Corbett, along with the saddlebags filled with his twenty-five thousand.

He'd left Duke in the livery stable after finding out from the man there that he owned it himself, with no partners. Maybe he paid protection to Baron and the sheriff, but at least they didn't own it.

He chose a small room with a comfortable bed, one that did not overlook the front of the house. He sat on the bed, hoping he'd made the right decision, the right judgment, about Boston Corbett. If the man did take off with his money, he'd have to hunt him down, but Corbett—if he did decide to abscond with the money—would have to start out on foot.

Clint had never gotten any indication from Corbett that he was larceny-minded. Of course, he hadn't seen the man in many years, but it seemed clear that if he was willing to steal to live, he wouldn't be living in a cave.

When delicious smells began wafting through the air from downstairs, Clint decided he'd given Olivia Lacy enough time to prepare something to eat, and he went back down. As he entered the kitchen, the combined smells—coffee and cooking meat of some kind—started his stomach growling.

"You're just in time," she said. "Sit down. You can start with coffee."

He sat at the table in the predominantly yellow kitchen, and she set a mug of steaming coffee in front of him.

"I hope you like beef stew," she said. "I always keep a large pot on the stove, just in case." She turned to face him, "As you can see, I am an eternal optimist."

"It works for me," he assured her. "Beef stew is one of my favorites."

"Well then," she said, "you'll love my beef stew, I can assure you."

She spooned it into a deep bowl and set it in front of him, then a basket with hunks of homemade bread. She gave him a large spoon and he started eating. She was right. Her beef stew was among the best he'd ever eaten.

"Do you mind if I join you?" she asked.

"Please," he said, "I'd enjoy the company."

She took a smaller bowl for herself and sat opposite him.

"What brings you to Concordia, Mr. Adams?"

"Well, I was here to play in a poker game."

"Are you a gambler by trade, then?"

"No, not at all," he said. "This was kind of a special occasion."

"And is your game over?"

"Yes, it is."

"I hope you won."

"Oh, I did," he said, "but it appears that in doing so I've made some enemies I didn't expect to make."

"May I ask who?"

"I think you know them," Clint said. "Mike Baron and Sheriff Reynolds. Apparently, I've walked into the middle of a business partnership I didn't know about."

"A lot of people have walked into that without knowing it," she said. "Why don't you just leave town?"

"I suppose I could do that, but Reynolds is the sheriff—crooked or not, he could still put a wanted poster out on me. I have enough problems without adding that to the mix. No, I've got to stay here and try to solve this problem, somehow."

"You could give the money back."

"I suppose I could," he said, dubiously.

"Is it a lot?"

"You know," he said, "this bread sops up the gravy real good."

She smiled.

"All right, that's none of my business," she said. "I hope you have it hidden somewhere safe," she said, then added quickly, "Oh my God, you didn't put it in the bank, did you?"

"I did," Clint said, "but I took it out again."

"That's good," she said. "You can't trust the bank manager, or the judge either."

"Tell me something, Olivia," Clint said. "Who can you trust in this town?"

"There are a lot of trustworthy people in Concordia, Clint. Unfortunately, none of them are in a position of power."

"What about elections?"

"I'm afraid those are well controlled, as well," she said.

"Sounds like a well-oiled machine operating here in Concordia."

"Yes," she said, "and only the few men at the top are getting oiled."

# THIRTY-TWO

The door to the judge's office opened and the bank manager, John Harvey, came in.

"About time," an annoyed Mike Baron said.

"Take it easy, Mike," Sheriff Reynolds said.

"Okay," Baron said, "now that we're all here, what are we gonna do about this problem?"

"This problem has a name," Judge McBride said. "Clint Adams. In case it has missed anyone's attention, that would be the Gunsmith."

"We know that, Judge," Reynolds said.

"I want to know," the judge said, "how Mike, here, thought it was a good idea to include the Gunsmith in his game. And then let him win. And then try to cheat him. How does any of that fit into what we're doing here?"

Reynolds looked at Baron.

"Mike," he asked, "you wanna try explainin' that to the judge?"

"He was recommended for the game," Baron said. "I

figured, okay, he's not a gambler, what are the chances he might win?"

"And, as it turned out, the chances were pretty good," the judge said.

"Look, a few players canceled and I had to replace them," Mike Baron said, "and the replacements were not very good."

"That was an error in judgment on your part," John Harvey said. "Why do we have to pay for that?"

"What did you have to pay for, John?" Baron demanded, angrily.

"Adams practically put a gun in my face."

"Well, he did the same to me!" Baron said.

"Mike, you told me he robbed you," the sheriff said. "He didn't."

"Well . . . almost."

Reynolds looked at Judge McBride.

"What can we get him on?" he asked.

"Well, almost robbing somebody is not a crime," the judge said.

"We can both testify that he threatened us, and robbed us," Baron said.

"I can say he robbed the bank!" Harvey said.

"We could do that," the judge said, "but he's a famous man. A trial would attract attention—media attention—from all over the country."

"We don't need that here," Reynolds said.

"No, we don't," the judge agreed. "In addition, I'm willing to bet our two friends here didn't keep their mouths shut about what happened. Did you?"

"Well . . . I told a few people," Baron said.

"I told my, uh, assistant," Harvey admitted.

"See?" the judge said to Reynolds. "They've already told people that Adams 'almost' robbed them. There's no way we can fit Adams for a frame."

"What's that leave?" Reynolds asked.

"That leaves it up to you, Sheriff," the judge said.

"I thought you'd say that."

"Well, come on, Reynolds," Baron said. "Whataya gonna do?"

"Well," Reynolds said, "I could kill one of you and frame Adams for that."

"What?" Harvey asked, alarmed.

"Relax, John," Baron said. "He's kiddin' . . . Aren'tcha, Sheriff?"

"That wouldn't work, Sheriff," the judge said, "because then we'd have to replace the one you killed."

"Okay," Reynolds said, "so that doesn't work."

Nervously, Harvey asked, "What else can you frame him for?"

"Well . . . I don't actually have to frame him for anything."

"Then what?" Baron asked.

"I can kill Adams," the sheriff said.

"That would attract even more attention than a trial," the judge said.

"Yeah, but nobody would be snooping around or checking out bogus charges," Reynolds said. "They'd just be comin' here to see the man who killed the Gunsmith."

"And who would that be?" the judge asked.

"Well, it just so happens we have another pretty famous man in town, who is already known for killin' someone."

"Who's that?" Baron asked.

"Fella named Boston Corbett."

"Who?"

"The man who killed John Wilkes Booth?" the judge asked.

"That's right."

"He's in town?" the judge asked.

"Well," Reynolds said, "not exactly in town, but he's close enough where we could frame him for killing Clint Adams."

"The man who killed John Wilkes Booth kills the Gunsmith," the judge said. "I like the way that sounds."

# THIRTY-THREE

"What about the mayor?"

Olivia looked at Clint over her coffee cup, which she was holding in both hands.

"What about him?"

"Is he as crooked as the sheriff and the judge and the banker?"

She frowned. "I'm not sure."

"He'd almost have to be, right? Or how could he be the mayor and deal with them?"

"I suppose so."

"So tell me, do you know an honest man in town who is in a position of authority?"

She thought a moment, then brightened. "I think I might."

"Who?"

"Jeff Spencer."

"And who is Jeff Spencer?"

"The editor of *The Concordia Gazette*," she said.

"The local newspaper," Clint said. "That's very good, Olivia. Do you know him?"

"I know him very well."

"Would you introduce me?"

"I'd be happy to."

"Now?"

"Right now?"

"Before it gets any later and he goes home."

"Actually," she said, "it might be better to see him at home. The newspaper office is right on Main Street. If you go in there, everyone will see you."

"And word will get back to the sheriff and the others," he said. "You're a very smart woman, Olivia."

"If I was," she said, "I'd be able to figure out a way to get out of this town, don't you think?"

"Why don't you just sell and move?"

"It's not that easy. The bank holds the note on this place, and I'm behind."

"I thought you said you weren't connected to any of them."

"I'm not," she said. "We have a second bank in town, which, to my knowledge, is not run by a crook. However, they could still foreclose on me if I don't pay."

"I see."

"Let's wait until just after dark," she suggested, "and then I'll take you to Jeff's house."

"We won't upset his family?"

"He doesn't have a family," she said. "He lives alone."

"Well, good," Clint said, then added, "I mean, good for me."

After dark they left Olivia Lacy's boardinghouse and walked to the home of the newspaper editor, Jeff Spencer.

Olivia knocked on the door. It was opened by a handsome man in his early forties who was very happy to see her, and then just as confused to see Clint with her.

"Olivia, what a pleasure," he said. "Who's your friend?"

"If you let us in, I'll tell you, Jeff," she said. "I think as a newspaperman you'll be very interested in what this gentleman has to say."

"All right, then," the man said, "come in."

They entered and followed Spencer to his living room.

"Can I get you something?" he asked. "Coffee? A drink?"

"Not for me, thanks," she said.

"Not for me, either."

"All right, then," Spencer said, looking at Olivia. "What's going on?"

"Jeff, this man's name is Clint Adams. He's staying at my house and—"

"Wait, wait," Spencer said. "Did you say . . . Clint Adams?"

Olivia looked confused. This was not the part she'd expected him to be interested in.

"That's right."

Now Spencer looked at Clint.

"The Gunsmith?"

"Yes."

"In Concordia? Without me knowing it?"

"I don't understand," she said, then suddenly it dawned on her, "Wait, did you say the Gunsmith?"

"You didn't know?" Spencer asked her.

"No, I had no idea." She looked at Clint. "Why didn't you tell me?"

"I don't go around announcing it," he said.

"Wait a minute, wait a minute," Spencer said. "This is

starting to make sense. I heard somebody new, somebody big was coming in to play in Baron's poker game. That was you?" He pointed at Clint.

"Yes."

"And I heard . . . you won?"

"That's right."

"And he's staying with you?"

"Yes," Olivia said.

"I think I need a drink," Spencer said.

"Okay," Clint said, "then I'll have one."

"You talked me into it," Olivia said. "I'll have one, too."

# THIRTY-FOUR

Spencer got them all situated with drinks and seated in the living room.

"Okay," he said, "what brings you to me?"

Clint told him about the poker game, what happened with Baron after he won, and then what happened with the sheriff and the bank manager.

"You're not gonna get any help from the judge, that's for sure," Spencer said, when he was done. "He's in deep with all of them."

"So I understand."

"Clint's looking for an honest man to talk to," Olivia said. "I suggested you."

"What about the mayor?" Clint asked. "Olivia says she doesn't know if he's in with them or not."

"He'd have to be," Spencer said. "I don't have anything on the mayor, but he'd have to be in with them, otherwise how are they getting away with what they're getting away with?"

"That's what Clint said," Olivia added.

"Okay," Clint said, "so what kind of help can I get from your newspaper?"

"What kind of help do you want?"

"You could write this story."

"As much as I'd like to," Spencer said, "I have to live in this town."

"Look," Clint said, "they're going to look for something to frame me for."

"Like what?" Spencer said.

"Well, what about Baron saying I robbed him?"

"I know Baron," Spencer said. "He's already told somebody what happened between you. They can't frame you for that."

"And the bank manager? Harvey?"

"John Harvey's a blowhard," Spencer said. "And he's already told somebody, too. No, they can't frame you for robbery."

"Then what?"

"I don't know," Spencer said. "Murder?"

"Murder of who?"

"They can just pick somebody out," Spencer said. "Anybody."

"Then there'd have to be a trial," Clint said. "People would come to town for that."

"You're right," Spencer said. "Too much attention."

"So you won't write it up the way I told you?"

"I can't, Mr. Adams," Spencer said. "Can you prove Baron tried to cheat you? That the sheriff—well, what did the sheriff do? Nothing that I can see."

"You're right," Clint said. "He hasn't done anything. Neither has the bank manager."

"So what can you do?" Olivia asked.

"Well, I can talk to the mayor, see what he has to say for himself."

"You'll have to listen carefully to what he says, how he says it, and then make up your mind as to whether or not he's with them."

"I know," Clint said. "Well, thanks for listening."

"Adams, I need something I can write where there won't be any reprisals. If they come after me, I need some leverage."

"I'll try and find out some."

Spencer walked them both to the door.

"By the way, where's the money?" he asked.

"It's safe," Clint said. "Someplace safe."

"Oh God, it's not in Olivia's house, is it?"

"No," Clint said, "that much I can tell you. It's not in her house."

# THIRTY-FIVE

The mayor's name was William Bartlett, and he agreed to see Clint when Clint presented himself to the man's assistant at city hall.

"Have a seat, Mr. Adams," the mayor said, from behind his desk.

He was tall, slender, in his forties, with black hair that came to a widow's peak. Clint thought the man looked nothing if not satanic.

He remained seated behind his desk and did not make a move to shake hands.

Clint sat, wondering if he would be able to put aside his inherent distrust of politicians.

"I'm aware of your reputation, sir," Mayor Bartlett said. "What brings you to Concordia? Oh wait, you played in Mike Baron's game, right?"

"That's right."

"Of course. And I heard you won."

"Right again."

"Well, congratulations," the mayor said. "Why are you still in town?"

"Your sheriff hasn't told you?"

"The sheriff and I don't speak every day," the mayor said, then smiled. "In fact, he and I don't speak every week."

"Don't you like him?"

"In a word, no," Bartlett said. "I don't think he's good for this town. Nor are his partners."

"Partners?"

"Mike Baron, John Harvey, and our good Judge McBride. Yes, they are all business partners."

"And you don't approve?"

"I say if they want to be partners, businessmen, that's what they should be. They should not have other interests, like being sheriff or judge, or even the bank manager. Someone might think they were using their positions to . . . well, feather their own nests?"

"I see."

"But you knew all this," the mayor said. "Let's put our cards on the table, so to speak, Mr. Adams. You're here to find out if I'm in with them."

"Why would I be here to do that?"

"That's what you're going to tell me. Otherwise, I have no idea why you're here. So either way, you'll have to enlighten me."

"Seems Mike Baron has accused me of robbing him," Clint said, "or, at least, coercing money out of him."

"I'm confused." The mayor frowned. "Didn't you win?"

"Yes, and he tried to cut a third of my winnings. When I suggested he take a smaller cut, he went to the sheriff to complain. Now your sheriff wants me to stick around town until he can 'solve' the dilemma."

"Were there any witnesses to this meeting where you were paid off?"

"No, he took me into his office to pay me off in private."

"Ah . . . Does Mr. Baron have a history of taking a large cut?"

"I don't know what his history is, but I intend to find out. The game was recommended to me by a friend. I'm going to have to do some checking of my own, find out just how much my friend actually knew about the game, and the host."

"And who would that friend be?"

"Bat Masterson."

"Oh yes . . . I know his reputation very well, too. Well, what do you propose I do about it?"

"I need an honest man in town," Clint said. "If they try to railroad me, I'm going to need help."

"I'm not exactly in a position to take sides, not at the moment, anyway," Mayor Bartlett said, "but I may be able to recommend someone who can. Of course, you'll have to trust me enough to take my recommendation."

"I realize that."

"Do you think you'll be able to do that?"

"I honestly don't know," Clint said. "I consider myself a good judge of character, but I also think you're a pretty good politician."

The mayor sat forward in his seat and said, "I'll take that as a compliment."

He wrote something on a slip of paper and pushed it over to Clint's side of the desk.

"Go and see this man," he said. "I believe you'll find he's honest to a fault."

Clint picked up the paper, put it in his pocket, and stood up.

"I'm obliged to you, Mayor."

"Mr. Adams," the mayor said. "I hope you'll make sure all your ducks are in a row before you decide to take any proactive measures."

"Not sure I know what you mean, Mayor."

The mayor smiled. "Don't kill anybody unless you know you're in the right."

# THIRTY-SIX

Clint left city hall, took out the slip of paper, and read it. The name on it was Woody Barnes. The address was literally two blocks away. He walked the two blocks, then looked up at the two-story brick building. There was a window on the second floor with writing on it. He backed up to read it. It said: "WOODROW BARNES, ATTORNEY-AT-LAW."

In Clint's opinion, lawyers were only slightly more trustworthy than politicians, but he went inside and walked up the stairs.

He entered the office, and found himself in an outer room with a desk but no secretary. A buildup of dust indicated there hadn't been a secretary in a while. He walked to the inner door and knocked.

"Come in!"

Clint entered, and left the door open behind him.

He entered. Behind the desk, right in front of the window, was a big, sandy-haired man in his thirties, clad at the moment in rolled-up shirtsleeves and suspenders. His jacket was draped over the back of his chair.

"Welcome, welcome, friend!" the man said, expansively. "Forgive the mess, but it's my secretary's day off."

"If we're going to start with bullshit, we're not going to get along at all," Clint said.

"You're right," Woody Barnes said. "The little lady left several weeks ago when I couldn't pay her back salary. What can I do for you, sir?"

"You were recommended to me by Mayor Bartlett."

Barnes laughed.

"Why is that funny?"

"If the mayor recommended me to you, it means you're up against it and you need someone who is used to fighting lost causes."

"I'm hoping that's not the case."

"Can we start with your name?"

"Clint Adams."

"Aha," Barnes said, "you've run afoul of the Concordia Machine, have you not?"

"The machine?"

"Sorry, my name for what Sheriff Reynolds, the judge, and their band of merry thieves have been doing. Have a seat."

Clint sat in an uncomfortable straight-backed wooden chair.

"Sorry, I need to buy more comfortable furniture."

"Tell me about the mayor. Is he on the level?"

"You mean is he in with Reynolds and that group? You know, I think Mayor Bartlett may be the only truly clean politician I've ever met."

"Then why doesn't he clean up his town?"

"He's a little outnumbered on the town council, and they are the ones who hire and fire in this town."

"Seems to me he could hire some help of his own to take care of it for him."

"If he did that," the lawyer said, "then he wouldn't be so clean, would he?"

"I suppose not."

"So he sent you to me," Barnes said. "He's hoping that you and me will get it done for him."

"I'm not looking to clean up the town," Clint said. "I just want to be able to take my money and leave without somebody putting a wanted poster out on me."

"Tell me what happened with the game."

Clint did. He felt like he was telling the story for the tenth time. He also told Barnes about the bank.

"Seems like you may be the first person to question Baron's cut of the game."

"Seems like it."

"Is the money safe?"

"Safe enough."

"What do you think they plan to do?"

"The easiest thing would be to kill me."

"That would mean an investigation."

"Conducted by Sheriff Reynolds," Clint said. "With my rep, they can put it down to someone wanting to make a name for themselves."

Barnes sat back in his chair. "What do you want me to do?"

"To tell you the truth, I don't know," Clint said. "I've been looking for somebody in this town who's honest. My search has taken me from Olivia Lacy to Jeff Spencer to Mayor Bartlett, and now to you. Now that I'm here, I guess I'll have to figure out what I need to do."

"Seems to me you need to be sure that neither Baron nor the bank manager tries to prefer charges against you."

"If they do, they have no witnesses, but since the judge is in on this, that wouldn't matter."

"Yeah, but they don't want national attention brought down on this place. They couldn't stand up against that kind of scrutiny," Barnes said. "Maybe what we need to do is make sure that kind of attention *does* come Concordia's way."

"And how do we do that?"

"I don't know," Barnes said. "I don't think we have anyone else in town who would be of that much interest to the rest of the country . . . do you?"

# THIRTY-SEVEN

"I suggest you don't spend much time alone," Barnes said before Clint left his office. "Come back and see me in the morning. Maybe one of us will have some ideas by then."

"I don't intend to be alone," Clint said.

He left the lawyer's office and walked back to Olivia's boardinghouse. She had a steak smothered in onions waiting for him. He was able to smell it outside the building.

"How did you know I'd be back in time?" he asked.

"I didn't," she said, with a smile. "This is for me. I was going to make yours when you got back, but since you're here . . ."

She put the steak on a plate and set it in front of him, then dropped one in the frying pan for herself.

"What happened with the mayor?"

"He sent me to Woody Barnes."

She turned quickly and stared at him.

"Barnes? He doesn't have a good reputation, Clint."

"What kind of reputation does he have?"

"He specializes in lost causes."

Clint stared at her. "I see what you mean."

She turned back to the stove.

Over supper Clint told her of his meeting first with the mayor and then with the lawyer.

"So you trust them?" she asked. "One of them, at least?"

"I naturally distrust lawyers and politicians," he said, "so this isn't going to be easy."

"So which one will you trust?"

"I'm inclined to go with Barnes. He doesn't seem to have anything to gain by working with the others."

"He's pretty much known as a loser," she said.

"Well, unless he's faking and he's a real good actor, that makes him number one in my book—well, number two."

"Thank you."

"I have one problem, though, that a lawyer really can't help me with."

"What's that?"

"I need someone to watch my back."

"You mean, with a gun?"

"Yes."

"I'm sorry Clint," she said. "I—I can't do that."

"That's okay," Clint said. "I might know somebody I can approach."

"Oh? Who?"

"Somebody else who's not quite what he seems to be," Clint said.

"Who would that be?"

"A man named Edgar Box."

"Box? Really? Edgar Box is around? Where did you meet him?"

"At the poker game. He was the only other person at the

table who seemed to know what he was doing, while seem-
ing not to."

"Another one?" she asked. "Isn't anybody who they
seem?"

"Well," he said, "there's me, and then there's you . . .
and I can't be all that sure about you."

"Touche," she said. "We *have* only just met. Maybe what
we need to do is . . . get better acquainted?"

"Actually," he said, "what I should probably do is leave
here. While I stay, I'm probably putting you in danger."

"I think, now that I know who you are, I can trust you to
look after me."

"Probably," he said. "It might take them a few days to
come up with a plan, and then somebody who can carry it
out."

"You mean they need to hire somebody to kill you?"

"That's what I mean."

It was up to Sheriff Reynolds to find somebody who could
and would kill Clint Adams. He sat in his office that night,
going through wanted posters on his desk. He didn't really
think he'd find somebody there, but maybe he'd find an
idea.

Boston Corbett was an idea, but he was a better choice
to pin the death of Clint Adams on then to actually carry it
out.

Of course, there was always Tessler.

Reynolds had sworn never to use Nick Tessler for a job
again. The man was hard—no, impossible—to control. And
how would he feel about killing the Gunsmith and not getting the credit for it?

He'd have to be paid enough money to make it worth it
to him.

Reynolds put the posters down and sat back in his chair. Two thousand ought to do it. Getting back the twenty-five would more than make up for it. And Tessler could always spread a rumor that he was the one who actually killed the Gunsmith.

Reynolds would send a telegram in the morning. Tessler was only one day away.

# THIRTY-EIGHT

Clint heard the floor outside his room creaking. He'd only been asleep about an hour, so when he came awake he was alert. He grabbed his gun from his holster and silently left the bed. He padded barefoot over to the door, stood beside it, and waited.

The floor creaked again. His room was on the wrong side of the house to get any moonlight through the window, but his eyes were used to the darkness.

Then someone was there, entering his room. He watched and waited. It was Olivia. She walked toward his bed, realized he wasn't in it, then looked around and saw him by the door.

"Did I frighten you?" she asked.

"Alerted me, is more like it." He lowered his gun.

"I'm sorry."

He walked to the lamp by his bed and turned up the flame just enough to bathe the room in a soft light.

"Is something wrong, Olivia?"

"No," she said, "I just wanted to ... . talk."

"About what?"

She walked to an armchair in the room and sat. She was wearing a robe over a nightgown. Her hair was down, and longer than he'd thought, the color of honey. She was prettier than he had noticed before, maybe because he was too busy with other things. She was also younger than he'd thought, probably not yet thirty.

"My husband died three years ago," she said. "He left me this house as a way for me to be self-sufficient. But it's been a struggle."

Clint sat on the bed and set his gun down. He was wearing only a pair of underwear, and suddenly became aware of that. He looked over at his shirt, hanging on the back of the chair she was seated on.

"I've been alone for three years," she said.

"By choice, Olivia?"

"Yes, actually," she said. "How did you know?"

"I think you would be faithful to a man forever, even if he was gone forever."

"He's not gone." She touched her breast. "He's in here. But sometimes he can't offer me any comfort . . . in here."

He got up, walked to the chair, and grabbed his shirt. He couldn't take it, though, because she was leaning against it.

"I just need—" he said.

"Sometimes," she said, touching his bare chest, "a woman needs another kind of comfort."

# THIRTY-NINE

"Olivia—" he said, warningly.

"Don't you find me . . . attractive?"

"Yes, of course I do," he said, "but I'm nobody to try to hitch your wagon to. I'll be gone from here in a few days."

"I know," she said, standing up. "That's the only reason I can do this. If I embarrass myself, I won't have to see you every day."

"Olivia," he said, as her hand moved over his stomach, "why would you embarrass yourself?"

"Well, I might embarrass myself if I try to undress myself," she said, "because my hands are shaking."

"Don't worry, then," he said in a soothing tone, "I'll take care of it."

He pulled the belt loose on her robe, peeled it down her shoulders and arms, and dropped it to the floor. She caught her breath when he took hold of the top of her nightgown and tugged it down. She gasped when her breasts bobbed free. He was surprised that they were kind of chubby, in spite of being small. Her tiny nipples began to swell, a rosy pink in color.

He cupped a breast in one hand while tugging the nightgown down the rest of the way with the other hand.

"There," he whispered, "you're naked."

"Oh my God, yes I am," she gasped.

"And you're beautiful."

He lowered his head, nursed one boob and then the other. She sighed, and let her head loll back as he suckled her nipples until they were nice and hard.

He walked her to the bed, then, laid her down gently, and removed his underwear. She gasped again when his erection came bobbing into view, long and hard and suffused with blood until it almost glowed red.

"Oh my . . ." she said, touching it gently, sliding her hand up and down the length of it. He put one hand on her breast and the other down between her legs. He fingered her until she was wet and gasping, then joined her on the bed.

"I don't want to wait," she said. "Don't be cruel to me."

He put his mouth to her ear and said, "I would never be cruel to you," and slowly slid his erection inside of her.

"Oh, yes, yes," she hissed, "oh God . . ."

There was only one man Reynolds intended to tell his plan to. He visited Judge McBride at his home late that night. The man was still awake, and had been drinking. The judge didn't sleep very well as he got older, and tended to drink too much at home, and hardly at all in public.

"Brandy?" he asked, showing the lawman into his study.

"Sure."

McBride closed the door.

"Emily is asleep," he said. "Damned if I can get more than a couple of hours a night anymore."

"I know what you mean."

The judge handed Reynolds a glass and said, "No, you don't. You're younger than me, and you live alone. If you can't sleep, it's because of things going on in your mind. I can't sleep because of things going on with my body."

Reynolds decided not to try and argue with the older man.

"Have a seat, Paul. What's on your mind?"

"Tessler."

"No," the judge said, "no, no, we said we'd never use him again."

"I know, but we don't have much time. What if Adams decides to leave town?"

"Then we'll put paper out on him."

"Yeah, but he'll still be gone, and so will the money," Reynolds argued. "No, we've got to get somebody to kill him now."

"But if we want to frame the hermit for it, will Tessler keep his mouth shut?"

"For a while," Reynolds said. "Long enough, anyway. By the time he does start talkin', it won't matter anymore."

"Paul . . ."

"Leave it to me, Judge," Reynolds said. "Don't I usually take care of everythin'?"

"Yes, you do, Paul," the judge said, "and you better take care of this one. Adams can blow everything we've been doing wide open."

"Tessler's the answer," Reynolds said. "I've heard how fast Adams is, but I've seen Tessler use a gun."

"Well, good God, man, he's not going to face him in the street."

"No, this will have to look like Adams was bush-whacked," Reynolds said.

"Well, make sure Tessler understands that," the judge said.

"He will."

"How much are you thinkin' of payin' the man?"

"Two thousand."

"That much?"

"We'll make it up when we get the twenty-five thousand back," the lawman said.

"Jesus," Judge McBride said, "Mike really messed it up this time. Didn't he know who Clint Adams was when he accepted him for the game?"

"He needed a big name when Masterson had to cancel," Reynolds said.

"Yeah, but a gambler, not a gunman," McBride said.

Reynolds finished his brandy and stood up.

"I'll take care of it, Judge."

"All right, Paul."

"I'll see myself out," the lawman said. "You just take it easy."

The judge nodded, his eyes drooping, and Reynolds left the study. He walked through the living room, but instead of continuing to the front door he turned and went up the stairs to the second floor. He entered the judge's bedroom, approached the bed, and looked down at the sleeping form of Emily McBride. At forty-four she was twenty years younger than her husband, a little older than the sheriff, not that he minded. She had a taut body, with firm hips and breasts, long legs, and the smoothest skin he'd ever encountered.

She was lying on her back, her nightgown askew, the sheet down to her waist. One nipple was peering out from behind her gown. He leaned over and licked it. She came awake immediately, with a gasp.

"Paul! Are you crazy?"

"Shhh," Reynolds said, "the judge is asleep in his study."

"Drunk?"

"Yes."

She smiled, and put her arms around his neck. "Then he'll be there for a while."

He lifted the nightgown up to her hips, ran his hand over her belly, and then down between her legs. She gasped as he pressed his fingers to her.

"I've been aching for you for days," she whispered.

"I told you," he said, "come to the office when you feel like that. We'll do it in a cell."

"And have your deputy walk in on us," she said. "Let's just do it now!"

He undid his gunbelt, then his trousers, and said, "You don't have to tell me twice."

# FORTY

Clint kissed the soft flesh of Olivia's thighs, and rubbed his face over her pubic hair so that she caught her breath again. The hair there as very light, almost whispy. When he licked her, the hair darkened and lay down immediately. He used his fingers to open her up, licked her where she was pink and smooth. Her body went taut as he continued to lick her, at the same time sliding one finger, and then two, in and out of her.

"Oh God," she said, as a wave of pleasure rolled over her. The tautness of her body broke and she began to thrash. He pressed his elbows down on her thighs to keep her pinned, continued to lick her while she went wild. Eventually, she became calmer, whimpered as he continued to lick her, and then she went taut and they repeated the process. He took her for a ride again, but this time right in the middle of it, he mounted her and drove himself inside of her.

Her eyes went wide, almost with shock. She wrapped her legs around him as he fucked her, her breath coming in harsh rasps in his ear.

He gathered her to him, slipping his hands beneath her to cup her buttocks, and since she had gone over the edge twice already, he closed his eyes, breathed her in, and went in search of his own explosion of pleasure and pain . . .

Reynolds rode the judge's wife so hard the bed squeaked and hopped up and down noisily. Luckily, the only time the judge did sleep soundly was when he was drinking and sitting in his chair.

Emily held onto Reynolds for dear life. He was younger and more virile then her husband, but no less selfish in the pursuit of his own pleasure. Still, he was better than nothing, and that's all the rest of the men in town had to offer her—nothing. She had tried a drifter from time to time, but they were no better, either. Coming off the trail after weeks or months, they took her like a whore.

No, Paul Reynolds was the best she could do for the moment. She held onto him, moved her hips, hoped that she'd reach some sort of climax before he finished, but it wasn't to be. He groaned, squirted into her, and immediately rolled off, and it was over.

"Why did you come by this late?" she asked, as he got dressed.

"I had somethin' to discuss with the judge."

"Is everything all right?"

"Of course," he said. "Why would you ask that?"

"The judge just seems to be . . . worried, lately," she said.

"He's just gettin' old," Reynolds said. He leaned down and kissed her. "I'll see you soon."

"All right."

He went off, very happy that he'd gotten to ease his own desires.

She tried to go back to sleep, but couldn't. Finally, she had to press her own hands down between her legs to get some relief . . .

Clint kissed Olivia and held her tightly in his arms.

"Can I stay here all night?" she asked.

"Of course."

"Can we do it again?" she asked, with a giggle.

He laughed and said, "Of course."

# FORTY-ONE

In the morning Sheriff Reynolds was at the telegraph office as soon as it opened.

"Kinda early for you, ain't it, Sheriff?" the key operator asked.

"Shut up, Ben," Reynolds said.

He grabbed a flimsy and began to write out his short message to Tessler in the nearby town of Bingam.

"Send it," he said, handing it to Carl, "and bring me the answer as soon as it comes in."

"Yes, sir."

Reynolds left the telegraph office and walked to his office. Once inside he put on a pot of coffee and sat behind his desk. They needed Clint Adams dead, and they needed it done fast. Now all he had to figure out was how to pin it on Boston Corbett, out in his cave. He'd have to talk to Tessler. Maybe they could grab Adams and take him out there to do it. Then all Reynolds would have to do is bring Corbett in and say that he shot Adams when Adams got too close to his cave.

This was going to work.

\* \* \*

Olivia slipped from Clint's grasp in the morning, kissed him, and said she was going downstairs to make breakfast. She told him to come down when he smelled coffee.

He rolled onto his back as she left the room. It had been quite a night, and he was sure the morning would be pleasantly spent over a good breakfast. After that, he didn't know what to expect from the day. He had a meeting with the lawyer, Woody Barnes, but he didn't have any fresh ideas. He hoped Barnes would.

When he smelled the coffee, he got up, got dressed, and went downstairs.

"You're dressed," she complained when he entered the office. She was wrapped in her robe, with no nightgown underneath. The effect was stimulating. "I thought maybe after breakfast we'd—"

"I have a meeting with Barnes, Olivia," he said. "We've got to try and figure a way out of this for me."

"Yes, of course," she said. "You want to solve your problem and leave town."

"Yes."

"Well, sit down," she said. "Have your breakfast, at least."

She gave him his coffee, then a plate of bacon and eggs.

"What about you?" he asked.

"I'm not very hungry."

"After last night?" he asked. "I sure worked up an appetite."

"I've lost my appetite," she said, glumly.

"Olivia, I'll be back later," he said. "I'll be spending the night here. I just don't know what will happen after that."

"I know."

"I told you last night—"

"I know!" she snapped.

She reached out and snagged a piece of bacon from his plate.

"I know," she said, more softly. "Don't worry. I'll be fine."

She reached for another piece, and he said, "Hey! I thought you lost your appetite."

"I changed my mind," she said, and got up to get herself some breakfast.

# FORTY-TWO

When Clint walked into Woody Barnes's office, the man was seated behind his desk, drinking coffee.

"Help yourself," Barnes said. "There's an extra cup there."

Clint walked over to the coffeepot, poured himself a cup, and carried it to a chair.

"Any bright ideas overnight?" Barnes asked.

"None," Clint said. "You?"

"One or two ideas," the lawyer said. "Don't know how bright they are. Wanna hear 'em?"

"Sure."

"One," Barnes said, "you leave town with your money and see what happens."

"And two?"

"Give me the money," Barnes said. "I'll put it in my account in the Farmer's Bank."

"That's the other bank in town?"

"That's right."

"They could still freeze my account, right? In that bank?"

"With a court order, yes."

"And they wouldn't have any trouble getting a court order."

"No," Barnes said.

"And what about your account?"

"They wouldn't have a good reason to freeze my account," the lawyer said.

"Do they need a good reason?"

"Whatever the judge does," Barnes said, "he might have to justify it in a federal court at some point, so they can't just pull a court order out of a hat. With you they can show some cause."

Clint thought about that.

"Unless the money is safe where it is?" Barnes said.

"It's safe."

"Then let's come up with another plan."

"I did have one thought."

"And what's that?"

"I need somebody to watch my back."

"With a gun?"

"Yes."

"Not me," Barnes said. "I'm terrible with a gun."

"There's a man I think I can approach," Clint said. "In fact, maybe two."

"Who are they?"

"They both played poker with me the other night," Clint said, "so it'll depend on whether or not they're still in town."

"Names?"

"Cole Weston and Edgar Box."

"Box? Really?"

"Yes, really."

"Well, let me check the hotels and see if they're still registered. If they're in boardinghouses, it may take a little longer."

"Not too long," Clint said. "If they're going to make a move on me, try to kill me, it'll be as soon as they can hire someone."

"They'll probably have to bring somebody in from out of town," Barnes said. "That would take until tomorrow. I would think we have at least that long."

"Okay."

"Meanwhile, keep a low profile."

"I can't make it seem as if I'm in hiding," Clint said. "That would bring the young guns out of the woodwork."

"Okay," Barnes said, "you know best when it comes to that."

"I'll be in touch," Clint said, getting up.

"Don't get killed today," Barnes implored. "We haven't even settled on my fee yet."

"I'm touched by your concern."

The sheriff looked up when the door to his office opened and the key operator, Carl, entered.

"Here's your reply, Sheriff."

"Thanks."

Reynolds took it from Carl, who turned and hurried out. He didn't like to be around Reynolds when he was in a bad mood.

Reynolds unfolded the telegram and read it. It was concise.

"BE THERE TOMORROW," it said, and was signed "TESSLER."

He folded it back up. Okay, the end was in sight. After this, Mike Baron was going to have to be very careful about who he invited into the game. Reynolds did not want to have to go through this again.

# FORTY-THREE

Clint knew that Barnes was checking to see where Edgar Box and Cole Weston were staying, but he decided to do some checking of his own. Obviously, they would have been at the Concordia House Hotel during the game, but once the game was over, they would have had to start picking up their own tab or move to another hotel. Or, of course, they could have left town.

Clint stopped in to the Concordia House, and the clerk flinched when he saw him.

"Mr. Adams," he said nervously, "I can't tell you anythin'—"

"Relax," Clint said, "I just want to know if somebody is staying here."

"Uh, who would that be, sir?"

"Cole Weston or Edgar Box," he said.

"They were both here during the game, of course, but Mr. Weston checked out right after."

"Did he move to another hotel?"

"I don't know, sir."

"What about Edgar Box?"

"He is still here, sir, and paying his own bill for the pleasure."

"I see. Is he in his room?"

"Yes, sir. In fact, he hasn't left his room since the game ended. I been sendin' his meals up to him."

"What room?"

"Sixteen."

"Thanks."

Clint went up the stairs to the second floor and walked down the hall until he came to room sixteen. He knocked and waited.

"Who is it?" Box's reedy voice asked.

"Clint Adams."

A few moments went by, then the lock turned and the door opened. Box peered out into the hall.

"It is you," he said.

"Yes."

"What do you want?"

"Can I come in?"

"If you're here to kill me, I warn you, I won't go easily."

"Why would I be here to kill you?" Clint asked. "I'm here to ask you for some help."

"Oh, well, come in, then."

Box opened the door and allowed Clint to enter. Clint noticed that the man was holding a pearl-handled .32-caliber gun.

"Who were you expecting?"

"One or more of those idiots from the game," the smaller man said. "I think they're still hanging around, waiting for me to step out onto the street."

"Well, if that's the case, maybe we can help each other."

"How so?"

Clint explained his trouble to Edgar Box, who listened intently.

"Well," Box said when Clint had finished, "maybe I should be happy I didn't win. I'm afraid I would have done the same thing you did and called him on his cut. But I still don't understand what you would like me to do."

"I need somebody to watch my back for a day or two, until I solve this problem. It sounds like you need the same thing."

"Hmm," Box said.

"I don't think any of those fellas from the game would try anything if I was with you."

"I think you're right," Box said, "but I have to tell you, I'm not a gunman."

"Can you hit anything with that thing?"

Box seemed to notice only then that he was still holding his gun, and he set it down on a nearby table.

"I can generally hit what I shoot at."

"Have you ever shot at a man?"

"On more than one occasion," Box said. "When you are my size, you sometimes have to prove yourself."

"Okay," Clint said, "I generally need to know more about somebody before I trust my back to him, but I don't seem to have a choice."

"Thanks for the glowing vote of confidence."

"Do you want to get out of this room or not?" Clint asked.

"Yes, I do. I'd like to go to a restaurant instead of eating here."

"Fine," Clint said. "Let's go. I'm not hungry, but I'll have some coffee and pie while you eat."

"That suits me," Box said. "Let's go."

He was wearing a shirt and tie, and he grabbed his jacket
and headed for the door.

"Box!"

"Yes?"

Clint looked at the gun on the table, thinking, I'm dead.

"Did you forget something?"

# FORTY-FOUR

"There he is," Pete Leslie said.

Mitchum raised his head from the hunk of wood he was whittling on. He wasn't making anything, just whittling.

"Who's that with him?"

"Damn," Leslie said. "Adams."

"Ha!" Mitchum said. "They're still running one-two."

"We gotta follow 'em," Leslie said. "They gotta split up sometime."

"Ya think?"

"You go tell Zack and I'll follow 'em."

"Yeah sure," Mitchum said. "Why not."

"That Johnny Reb ain't gettin' away," Leslie said. "Zack feels the same."

"And so do I," Mitchum said, "but I ain't goin' against the Gunsmith, no matter what."

"Just go!" Leslie said.

"Sure."

Mitchum dropped the hunk onto the pile of shavings.

* * *

Nick Tessler rode into Concordia, Kansas, early that same morning. He hadn't been there in over a year, but the promise of two thousand dollars had lured him, no questions asked. He didn't care who he had to kill to make the two thousand.

Tessler was the kind of man who drew attention just by riding in. Today was no different. Men and women on both sides of the street stopped to look. Tessler kept staring ahead, but suddenly he had the urge to turn his head and look, and he locked eyes with a man.

Edgar Box watched Clint lock eyes with the man on the horse.

"Know him?" he asked.

"I know his type," Clint said.

Box looked at the man, and then beyond him. He saw Pete Leslie also staring at the man, and Hank Mitchum skulking away. Looked like throwing in with Adams had already saved him some trouble.

The rider moved on.

"I think I already know who they brought in to take care of me," Clint said.

"But you don't know him?"

"Never saw him before."

"He seemed to know you."

"He recognized me, but he doesn't know me."

"Too confusing for me," Box said. "Leslie and Mitchum were across the street."

"I saw them," Clint said. "Leslie will follow up. Mitchum is probably going to get Foxx." Clint looked at Box. "You still hungry?"

"Famished."

"Let's go."

* * *

They stopped at a small café Clint had never been to before. Box ordered the beef stew. Clint didn't bother telling him that he'd already had better.

He ordered a slice of peach pie and some coffee.

"Leslie's across the street," Box said, with his mouth full.

"He'll wait for the other three."

"And then what?"

"Then they'll wait to see if we split up when we leave here."

"But we won't, right?"

"Nope."

After a few moments of silence Box asked, "So that's the man I have to watch your back against?"

"Him and whoever else he gets to stand with him—if they stand."

"What else would they do?"

"Bushwhack me."

"What would they accomplish with that?" Box asked. "Shooting you in the back, how does that enhance anyone's reputation?"

"Killing me enhances a rep," Clint said. "Nobody has to know how they did it."

"Witnesses."

"After a few weeks, stories fade and change. But I don't think that's going to matter here. I think he's getting paid to kill me, and the method doesn't really matter."

"So what if they shoot us both in the back?"

"That's not supposed to happen, if we're watching each other."

"Um, yeah, about that . . ."

"I have an idea."

"What?"

"Finish eating, and we'll go see if Cole Weston has left town yet."

# FORTY-FIVE

Tessler entered Sheriff Reynolds's office without a word. Reynolds looked up from his paperwork.

"Tessler."

"So?" Tessler asked. "Where's my money?"

Reynolds opened a drawer, took out an envelope, and tossed it to the man, who caught it neatly.

"Half?" he asked.

"All of it, up front," Reynolds said.

"Who's my target?"

"Clint Adams."

Tessler's face brightened, something Reynolds had never seen.

"That's who it was."

"You saw him?"

Tessler nodded.

"On the street," he said. "He was walking with a small man."

"Edgar Box."

"Box?"

"Don't tell me you know him."

"I know the name," Tessler said.

"A gambler?"

"That's not what I know him for. Is he part of the deal?"

"Only if he gets in the way."

"How do you want this done?"

"From behind."

"What?"

"We're going to pin it on someone else."

"I get no credit?"

"That's why I doubled your price," Reynolds said. "You can claim credit later—much later. Just not right away. Okay?"

Tessler hefted the envelope full of money, then said, "All right. When do you want it done?"

"As soon as possible."

"Today?"

"That's soon enough."

Tessler shook his head.

"The Gunsmith," he said. "What a kick it would be to face him in the street."

"Tessler—"

"I know, I know," Tessler said. "Don't worry. I'll keep my end of the bargain."


"What's Box doing with Adams?" Foxx asked, as he walked down Main Street with Mitchum.

"Damned if I know," Mitchum said. "Maybe they're watching each other's back. We can't go after Box while Adams is with him."

"When did Clint Adams become a Southern sympathizer?" Foxx asked.

"I don't know."

"Damn!"

They kept walking until they saw Leslie waving at them. They stepped into a doorway with him.

"They're in that café across the street."

"Think they'll separate when they come out?" Mitchum asked.

"I don't know," Leslie said.

"If they don't, we can't touch him," Foxx said. "Not yet."

"I didn't get the impression they even liked each other," Mitchum said.

"Perhaps," Zack Foxx said, "they just need each other."

"Why Weston?" Box asked. "He seemed rather . . . self-centered to me."

"He is," Clint said, "but if we can motivate him, he'll be useful."

"What have you got to motivate him with?"

"We just have to pique his interest."

"Or?"

"Offer him money."

"You have money."

"That's right."

"Isn't this all about getting you out of town with the money?" Box asked. "Why offer him some?"

"Because I'd rather get out of town with most of the money than none of it."

"I suppose I can see that."

"Finish eating," Clint said. "We've got three men across the street who will probably follow us."

"They're not very good at following, are they?"

"I think the point is simply to follow, and not necessarily to do it unseen. They probably want you to think about it."

"I see."

"I have a question."

"Yes?"

"Were you really a Southerner?"

"I was born in the South," Box said, "but I haven't been back home in a long, long time."

"And were you in the war?"

"No."

"Then you just brought that up to bait them?" Clint asked.

"I thought it might bait one of them," Box said, "not all three."

"So you got more than you bargained for."

"Don't we always get more than what we bargain for?" Box asked. "That's what makes life so interesting."

"I have never had much trouble keeping my life interesting."

"No, I guess not," Edgar Box said, pushing away from the table, "not if even half of what I've heard about you is true."

"Half," Clint said, thoughtfully. "At this point in my life I guess that'd be about right."

# FORTY-SIX

When Clint and Box left the café, they hesitated just outside. The three men across the street hoped they would go their separate ways, but the two men finally turned in the same direction and walked off together.

"Damn," Foxx said.

"We might as well follow 'em," Leslie said. "I'm sure Adams has seen us."

"He's not just gonna stand by and let us follow him," Mitchum said.

"Why not?" Leslie asked. "He probably knows we're not after him. What does he care how long we follow him?"

"We could just forget the whole thing," Mitchum suggested.

Foxx looked at him.

"Aren't you the one who said that damned Southerner had to pay?"

"Well, yeah, but not Adams . . ."

"Then we'll just wait for our chance," Foxx said.

"How long?" Mitchum asked.

"As long as it takes."

Clint and Box walked to the office of Woody Barnes.

"A lawyer?" Box asked.

"I needed somebody in this town who wasn't connected to Reynolds, Baron, and the judge."

"And are you sure he's not connected?"

"Pretty sure."

"How sure?"

"About seventy-five percent sure."

"Is that good enough?"

"For now."

They went inside.

Barnes looked up as the two men entered his office.

"There you are. I found out your buddy Edgar Box is staying at the Concordia."

"Woody Barnes," Clint said, "meet Edgar Box."

"Nice to meet you," Barnes said.

"Likewise."

"What about Weston?" Clint asked. "Is he still in town?"

"You mean you didn't find him on your own?"

Clint just stared at him.

"Yeah, okay, he's stayin' at the Bedford, over on West Street."

"Okay," Clint said.

"So Mr. Box has agreed to help?"

"We're helping each other, Woody," Clint said.

"So you don't need me to do anything else right now?" Barnes asked.

"Just stand by, Woody," Clint said. "I get the feeling things are coming to a head quickly."

He and Box turned and walked out.

Nick Tessler checked into a fleabag hotel in a low-life part of town, because that's where he felt comfortable. He liked people who were down on their luck; he liked whores who had some mileage on them. In other words, he liked people he could look down on.

And this was also the part of town where he'd find himself some cheap, throwaway labor. A quick fifty dollars to someone who didn't need to come out the other end alive.

Disposable help.

The Bedford Hotel was a step down from the Concordia House Hotel. Clint and Box entered the lobby and approached the front desk.

"What room is Cole Weston in?"

"Mr. Weston is in room . . . two-fourteen, sir."

"Thanks."

Clint and Box went up the stairs and walked to room two-fourteen.

Clint knocked, and when Cole Weston answered he looked like a mess. He had obviously been holed up in the room drinking, for a long time.

"Hey, boys," he said, "come on in and have a drink."

# FORTY-SEVEN

The room was as much of a mess as the man was. The sheets were off the bed, there were whiskey bottles everywhere, and his shirt was so soiled he probably hadn't changed it since the night of the game.

"Bring any whores with ya?" Weston asked. "I ran outta whores."

"Jesus, Weston," Clint said, "what have you been doing in here?"

"Well, I tol' ya I run out of whores," Weston said, "so whataya think I been doin'?"

Edgar Box looked as if he was afraid he'd catch something if he was there too long. He stayed near the door.

Weston was standing in the middle of the room, weaving, unsteady on his feet. He spotted a whiskey bottle that still had some liquid at the bottom, but as he reached for it he fell over, landing on his back across the bed.

"Jesus, Adams," Box said, "we're not going to get any help out of him."

"I know it," Clint said. "Come on."

Edgar Box couldn't get the door open fast enough.

Outside, the two men Tessler had chosen were standing in front of the hotel, waiting. The fifty bucks he'd paid was burning a hole in each man's pocket. They couldn't wait to get this over with and get to the saloon, and then a whorehouse.

Tessler was on the roof across the street with a rifle, ready to earn his two thousand.

Clint and Box stepped out of the hotel and came face-to-face with the two waiting men.

"You Adams?" one of them asked.

"That's right."

"We got business with you."

"I don't have any business with you," Clint said.

"That don't matter," the second man said. He looked at Box. "This ain't got nothin' ta do with you, mister."

"Fine by me," Box said, moving aside.

"You boys are making a big mistake," Clint said. He wanted to look at the rooftops across the street, but he dared not take his eyes from the two men in front of him. Also, he didn't want to underestimate them, just because they looked like they had recently gotten up from sleeping in the street.

The two men knew they were facing the Gunsmith, but they also knew that Tessler had told them that Adams would be dead well before he could draw his gun.

However, they were now wondering why Adams wasn't dead yet. Their job was only to distract him.

"Well?" Clint asked. "What are you waiting for?"

The two men flexed their fingers nervously, sensing that they may have been duped.

"Mister—"

Suddenly, Edgar Box drew his gun and fired up at the roof across the street. His .32-caliber bullet traveled straight and true and hit Nick Tessler in the forehead. Tessler dropped his rifle off the roof, then fell over and joined his rifle on the ground below.

The two men jumped nervously, and then snatched at their guns. Clint calmly drew, fired twice, and dropped them both onto their backs.

Clint and Box both ejected their spent shells and reloaded before moving or speaking.

"That was a hell of a shot with that caliber gun," Clint said.

"As long as you hit what you aim at, I've found any gun does the job," Box said, "but I like this one."

Clint checked the two men he'd shot. They were dead. Then he walked across the street and checked on the third man. Also dead, and he realized it was the man who had ridden into town that morning. He would have had a better chance if he'd faced Clint in the street.

Clint returned to the front of the hotel, where Box was waiting.

"Now what?" Box asked.

"I suppose that's up to you."

"What do you mean?"

"You're better with that gun than you are with a deck of cards," Clint said. "I'm thinking your true reason for being in town hasn't come out yet."

Box looked thoughtful, then said, "Yeah, you're right. I came here to try you myself. I didn't think he'd get to it before me."

"You know him?"

"Looks like a man named Tessler."

"Don't know him," Clint said. "Don't know you, either."

"I guess one of us thought we'd get known by killing you—except I decided to first see if I could beat you at the poker table."

"Well," Clint asked, "since that didn't work out, what's your next move?"

The two men stood facing each other, each of their guns holstered. People had gathered around for the sake of the action, and were now wondering if there was more to come. Standing at the edge of the crowd was Sheriff Reynolds.

"Seems to me you got enough problems hereabouts without me adding to them," Box said.

"I think my troubles may be over," Clint said, "if this was their best try at me."

"Think it was?"

Clint turned, and saw the sheriff slinking away.

"I think that's what they're going to have to decide," Clint said.

"Well," Box said, "then you don't need me anymore. I think I'll go looking for greener pastures."

"Sounds like a good idea," Clint said. "I'll probably be doing that myself."

"Maybe we'll run into each other some other time," Box said.

"It might be a good idea if we didn't," Clint said.

Box touched his hat brim, turned, and walked away . . .

# FORTY-EIGHT

"Wait a minute," Sheriff Pete McKay said. "That can't be the end of the story."

"Pretty much," Clint said. "The sheriff had a meeting with his partners and they decided I should leave town."

"With the money?"

Clint nodded. "They decided to absorb the loss."

"And they went on running their game?"

"For a few months. But I heard they tried to cheat the wrong man, again, only this time he had a gang with him. The gang cleaned Concordia up without really meaning to, and left town. They had elections to fill the vacancies created by the dead men, and there were no more poker games in that town."

"And Edgar Box? I've never heard of him. What happened? Did those three men finally get him?"

"No, I think they saw him make that shot that day and changed their minds. They left town even before I did. I heard Box was shot and killed a few weeks later when he went up against somebody faster."

"And what about your money?"

"Well," Clint said, "I rode back out to Boston Corbett's cave and guess what I found?"

"He lit out with your money."

"He lit out, all right, but my money was still there," Clint said.

"All of it?"

"Every cent," Clint answered. "Corbett didn't take a dollar."

"Didn't leave a note?"

"I don't think he had anything to write with."

"So why'd he leave?"

"I think he felt the change in the wind thereabouts, figured it was time to move on."

"And you never ran into him again until now?"

"Never saw him, never heard a thing about him. I figured he was dead, somewhere. How did he end up in that place?"

"All I know is he was working as the assistant door-keeper at the Kansas House of Representatives when, one day, he walked into the assembly and started shooting."

"Kill anybody?"

"No, he was firing into the air."

"Why did he start shooting? Any idea?"

"I heard he thought the morning prayer was being mocked."

"Never knew him to be religious."

"Well, he was arrested, tried, found insane, and sentenced to the asylum."

Clint shook his head.

"I guess he should have stayed in that cave."

"Well," the sheriff said, "thanks for the stories. I think I'll get some shut-eye."

"Me, too," Clint said. "Maybe, with a little luck, we can still catch up to him before he gets a horse."

"Do you think he'll recognize you when we catch up to him?" the lawman asked.

"I don't know," Clint said. "Do you think you'd recognize a man who trusted you to watch over twenty-five thousand dollars about ten years ago?"

"I'd remember anyone who trusted me with twenty-five dollars," McKay said. "See you in the mornin'."

Clint nodded.

"I'm going to finish this coffee and turn in."

The sheriff went and wrapped himself in his blanket, tilting his hat down over his eyes.

Clint hadn't thought about Boston Corbett very much since Concordia. Hadn't thought about Edgar Box much, either. Now Box was dead, and Corbett was insane—or was he?

# FORTY-NINE

Lieutenant Cooper made himself useful by making the coffee in the morning. He handed McKay a cup while Clint checked on Eclipse.

"I was listening to Adams tell you his stories last night," he said.

"Sorry we kept you awake."

"Not what I meant," Cooper said. "Are you sure he should be comin' along with us?"

"Coop, I'm not sure you should be comin' along with us," McKay said. "There's no harm in havin' along somebody who knows Corbett. He may listen to reason."

"This is the only reason I'm gonna give him," Cooper said, touching the gun he wore high on his hip in a cavalry-type holster.

"There's not gonna be any reason to shoot this man, Cooper," McKay said. "He ain't even armed."

"He could be armed and on a horse by now," Cooper reasoned.

"Still no reason to plan on shootin' him," McKay said. "Don't forget he's the man who shot Booth and avenged Lincoln."

"You're talkin' to the wrong man," Cooper said. "I'm from South Carolina."

"I don't care, Coop," McKay said. "You keep that gun holstered until I say, understand?"

Cooper pushed out his lower jaw.

"You ain't in charge here, Sheriff."

"Yeah, I am," McKay said. "You weren't invited. But even if you were in charge, I don't think Adams would like it if you shot Corbett on sight. You might have some explainin' to do to him."

"What kind of explaining?" Clint asked, approaching the fire.

McKay saw the concerned look on Cooper's face as he looked up at Clint.

"I was tellin' Cooper he's gonna have to explain to you about this weak coffee."

"Weak coffee can get you shot," Clint told Lieutenant Cooper. "Toss in an extra handful or two in the future."

"I'll remember," grumbled Cooper.

Director Desmond took one more look at the missive he'd received from the governor, then looked up as the door to his office opened.

Ed Frame was his head orderly, but Frame had a background of being able to handle a gun.

"Did you get them?" Desmond asked.

"I've got four men goin' with me," Frame said. "Two orderlies and two men from town."

"That's good," Desmond said.

"Are you sure about this?" Frame asked.

"I've got the word from on high," Desmond said. "Get it done."

"You know, when I took this job, I thought I left my gun behind," Frame said.

"This is going to pay very well, Mr. Frame," Desmond said, "and it is of importance to those of us who still support the South."

"The war's over, Mr. Director."

"Not for me," Desmond said, "not for the governor."

"The governor's behind this?"

Desmond stood up.

"All you need to know is what I've told you, Mr. Frame," Desmond said. "Boston Corbett, 'Lincoln's Avenger,' must not return here alive. Understood?"

"Understood," Frame said, "but I won't be doin' this for some misguided belief that the South will rise again. I'm doing this for money."

"And you'll get it," Desmond said. "That's a promise."

After coffee and some jerky—Cooper complaining about beef jerky for breakfast—they saddled up and mounted.

"He always such a complainer?" Clint asked McKay as Cooper rode ahead.

"He wants to be in charge," McKay said. "Ever since he joined the police department, he thinks he's better than his old boss."

"He used to be your deputy?"

"For a while," McKay said. "When they decided to have a police department, he ran and applied."

"They took him and made him a lieutenant?" Clint asked. "That bother you?"

"No," McKay said. "He was a decent enough deputy, but he really ain't so much as a lieutenant."

"You think he's been sent with us to kill Corbett?" Clint asked.

McKay gave Clint a quick look.

"I heard what you were talking about," Clint said.

"Everybody around here but me eavesdrop?" McKay wondered. "Naw, I don't think he's been sent, but it wouldn't surprise me if they send somebody. We got a lot of Southerners in town who ain't yet admitted that the war is over."

"You know, I ran into this in Concordia, and a lot of other places," Clint said. "How do so many Southerners end up in positions of power?"

"Must be natural politicians," McKay said. "We better catch up to him. He's goin' the wrong way."

# FIFTY

"I got 'im!"

"What?" McKay asked.

"You lookin' fer that escaped outlaw?" Lem Smith asked.

"We're looking for an escaped patient from a hospital," Clint said.

"Well, I got 'im. Come on. I 'spected you'd be comin' along eventual-like, Sheriff."

They had ridden up to Lem Smith's ranch because that was the first place they came to traveling in the direction Boston Corbett had led them. Smith had come running out when he saw them riding up. He was holding an ancient Winchester in his hands.

He led them to his barn, removed a rusty padlock from the front doors, and opened it. There, sitting in the center of the floor, was Boston Corbett, looking very different from the last time Clint had seen him. Gone were the long hair and beard, as well as the coating of dirt. He was shorn, and still wearing his hospital whites. His chin was down on his chest, as if he'd been sleeping. When he saw Clint, he asked, "Did you find your money?"

They had a meal in Lem Smith's house, served by his wife. Clint wanted to bring Corbett inside to eat, but Smith's wife, Hazel, wouldn't have it.

"Don't care if he escaped from a prison or a hospital, don't want him in my house," she said.

"I'll take a plate to him, if you don't mind," Clint said.

She frowned, looked as if she was about to dig her heels in.

"We need him to keep his strength up for the ride back, Miz Smith," McKay said, quickly.

"Well, awright," she said.

She fixed a plate and handed it to Clint. It was some kind of stew, and while he ate it and enjoyed it, Clint didn't want to know what the meat was.

He left the house and walked to the barn, undid the padlock and entered. Boston Corbett was still seated in the center of the room, his legs manacled so closely together he would not be able to walk. The farmer seemed to have an unusual collection of padlocks and chains. Clint had to remove a pair of wrist manacles so Corbett could eat.

"Thanks," Corbett said. "I'm not crazy, you know."

"I didn't think you were."

"Even when I was livin' in a cave?"

"Hey, that worked out for me," Clint said. "It was a good place to hide my money."

"Why did you ever trust me with that money?" Corbett asked.

"I told you then, you were an honorable man. You didn't even take a dollar. You proved me right."

Around a mouthful of stew, Corbett asked, "How much was in them saddlebags anyway?"

"Twenty-five thousand," Clint said. "You never looked?"

"Never did," Corbett said. "Guess I shoulda took a ten."

"Or a twenty."

Corbett had consumed half the stew, and Clint handed over his canteen so the man could wash it down.

"What the hell are you doin' here, anyway?" Corbett asked.

"I was in town, heard your name, and figured to check it out."

"Surprised at what you found, huh?"

"Not after finding you in a cave about ten years ago," Clint said. "Boston, what were you thinking shooting up the House?"

"Those idiots!" he snapped, then he softened and said, "I don't wanna talk about it."

"Fine, we won't talk about it."

"What are you gonna do with me?"

"Take you back."

"Everybody knows who I am by now," he said. "Some Southern sympathizer who doesn't know the war is over is gonna try to kill me. I shot their patron saint."

"Yeah, I guess you did. Don't worry, I'll get you back safe."

"And then what?" he asked. "That director's got a Southern accent. Mark my words, he'll make sure I die in my room."

"I'll talk to the governor about getting you out," Clint promised.

Corbett made a rude sound with his mouth and said, "Another Southerner."

Clint realized the man was right.

"Look," he promised, "I'll talk to the director when we get back. If I'm not convinced that you're safe, I'll break you out myself."

Boston Corbett finished his stew and handed the bowl back.

"Better chain my wrists again. Don't want you gettin' in trouble on my account."

"Even with your hands free, you'd still have to hop to get away," Clint said. "I'll take the chance."

# FIFTY-ONE

Ed Frame and his men had an easier time of it. They didn't have to track a man who was on foot. Rather, they were tracking Clint, McKay, and Cooper.

"They're headin' for Lem Smith's place," Dooley Wilkins said.

Dooley lived in town and knew everybody, so Frame had no reason to doubt him. They decided to camp the night and then take a look at Lem Smith's place.

"We ain't thinkin' about takin' on the Gunsmith face-to-face, are we?" Tom Lawford, one of the orderlies, asked. "I mean, I ain't no gunhand, Frame."

They were all seated around the fire, drinking coffee and eating beans.

"We don't have to face Adams as all," Frame said. "All we got to do is make sure Boston Corbett don't get back to Edgewood."

"By killin' him?" Ben Croft asked. He was the other orderly Frame had recruited.

"That's about the only way I can think of," Frame said.

"You know," Lawford said. "Corbett ain't a bad guy. He's kinda interestin'."

"You know what I find interesting?" Arlo Huff asked. He was the second man from town Frame had hired. "Money. That's about the only thing I find interesting."

"Hey," Dooley said, "if we gotta kill this crazy man, we gotta kill him. That's it."

"He ain't crazy," Croft said. "Not really."

"Then what was he doin' in that crazy house?" Arlo demanded.

"It ain't a crazy—" Lawford started, but Frame cut him off.

"Forget it, Tom," he said. "They ain't gonna get it. Look, we got a job to do, so why don't we just do it?"

"Yeah, but maybe—" Croft started.

"And stop talkin' about it!" Frame said. "Ben, go see if the horses are okay. And we're gonna set watches. There are enough of us that we'll each get plenty of sleep. Dooley, you first."

"And what exactly are we watching for?" he asked.

"Just the off chance that Adams and the sheriff might decide to head back at night."

When Clint came back from feeding Corbett, McKay was waiting on the front porch, smoking a cigarette.

"Did you take off his manacles?" he asked.

"Just the ones on his wrists," Clint said. "He's not going anywhere."

"Not the way ol' Lem's got his legs trussed up, he ain't," the sheriff agreed.

"He seems resigned to going back, and being killed," Clint said.

"So what do you want to do? Give him some money and a horse?"

"That's not what I signed on to do," Clint said. "I'll keep to my word and bring him back."

"That's good," McKay said, "because if you wanted to let him go, I know there's nothin' I could do to stop you. You could probably kill me and Cooper without breaking a sweat."

"I don't kill lawmen," Clint said.

"That's good to hear," McKay said. "But watch out for Cooper."

"Watch out for what?"

"I don't think he's as determined to bring Corbett back alive as we are."

"Is he a killer?"

McKay hesitated.

"Cooper's . . . odd," McKay said. "I think he'd do just about anything to get ahead, so if he thought killing some-one would help him, he'd do it."

"It wouldn't matter who?"

"I don't think Coop would look past his own wants," McKay said.

"You're pretty insightful for an old-time, Old West law-man."

"Topeka is not like a lot of the Old West Kansas towns of the past," McKay said. "If I want to keep my job a while longer, I have to change with the times. That means I can't always be reachin' for my gun at the first sign of trouble."

"I get it."

"I think you and me should bunk in the barn with Cor-bett, just in case," McKay said, flicking his cigarette into the darkness.

"Sounds good to me," Clint said. "My bedroll's already in there with the horses."

"And you really don't think, with his hands clean, that Corbett's gonna try to get on a horse?"

"He can't spread his legs," Clint said, "and the doors are padlocked."

Cooper came rushing out of the house suddenly, and stopped when he saw the two of them.

"What's your hurry, Coop?" McKay asked.

"I, uh, just thought I should bunk in the barn with you fellas."

"I don't think so," Clint said.

"What? Why not?"

"Because I won't sleep real well with you in there, that's why," Clint said.

"You got no say, Adams—" Cooper started, but McKay cut him off.

"But I do," he said. "Adams and I will bunk in with Corbett. You sleep in the house."

Cooper looked like he wanted to argue further, but he was outnumbered and finally saw that.

"Fine!" he said, and stormed into the house.

"That didn't help much."

"Whataya mean?"

"I'm probably still not gonna sleep real well with him around."

"Well then," McKay said, "I guess we're just gonna have to take turns keepin' watch."

# FIFTY-TWO

Ed Frame broke camp in the morning. He called Arlo Huff over.

"You scout ahead, Arlo."

"For what?"

"If Adams and the sheriff found Corbett, they'll be on the way back," Frame explained. "We don't want to blunder headlong into them."

"Okay."

"If you see them, don't engage them, just come back and tell us so we can get ready for them."

"Gotcha."

Huff mounted up and rode on ahead.

"What's he doin'?" Ben Croft asked.

"He's doing what he's told," Frame said, "which is what you boys ought to start doing."

"I done what you said," Croft argued.

"That fire is still smoldering," Frame said. "When I said put it out, I expected you to put it out!"

Frame stormed over to the fire and stomped it completely out.

Clint was keeping the last watch, peering out through a crack in the door, when Sheriff McKay awoke. Clint looked over at the sleeping form of Boston Corbett as the lawman struggled to his feet and approached him.

"Mornin'," McKay said.

"Good morning."

"Anything happenin' outside?"

"Mr. and Mrs. Smith are up and going about their day," Clint said. "We should get out of their way."

"We'll have to borrow a horse from them."

"I think they'll go along with that."

"Seen Cooper?"

"Not yet."

"We better wake him up," McKay said. "I'll go get him, and you get Corbett together."

"Okay."

"We're still takin' him back, right?"

"Of course," Clint said. "Nothing's changed just because we had a night's sleep."

"Okay," McKay said.

"Corbett and me will saddle the horses," Clint said.

"Right."

As McKay walked to the house, Clint went over to Corbett and woke him. Corbett rolled over and looked up at Clint.

"Time to get going," Clint said.

"Right."

Clint put his hand out and helped Corbett to his feet, then removed the shackles from his ankles.

"Let's get these horses saddled," Clint said.

"We gonna have any food?"

"I'll give you some beef jerky as soon as the horses are saddled."

Corbett nodded. By the time McKay returned with Cooper, the horses were ready. But the two lawmen didn't come back the way Clint had expected.

"Adams."

Clint turned, and looked at the two men standing in the doorway. Cooper had his gun on McKay. The sheriff had been disarmed.

"What's going on?"

"He got the drop on me when I walked in," McKay said. "Sorry."

"Move away from Corbett and the horses," Cooper said.

Clint knew if he moved, Cooper would have a clear shot at Corbett.

"What are you going to do, Cooper?" Clint asked. "Once you kill Corbett, you going to kill us, too?"

"I just need to finish Corbett," Cooper said. "Then I'll ride back and get prepared for you two."

"I see," Clint said. "You'll pin the killing on us."

"I'm just gonna do my job."

"And what job is that, Coop?" McKay asked.

"Doing what I'm told."

"With no questions asked?" McKay asked. "Is that still the way you think you'll get to the top?"

"Yeah," Cooper said, "then it'll be tellin' other people what to do."

"That's your goal?" Clint asked. "To be able to give orders?"

"I'm tired of takin' 'em all the time," Cooper said.

"So quit," McKay said. "Go back to wearin' a badge."

"Yeah, right," Cooper said. "Nobody tells you what to do, right?"

"Coop—"

"Shut up!" Cooper said, digging the barrel of his gun into the sheriff's side. "Move, Adams, or I'll put a bullet in the sheriff."

"Would he do that, McKay?" Clint asked.

"Yeah," McKay said, "he's just stupid enough to do it."

"Well, then, you better drop."

"Wha—" Cooper asked, but suddenly McKay went limp and hit the ground.

Clint hated trick shots. When he shot, he shot to kill, but he had never killed a lawman in his life. At least, not one that hadn't turned. At that moment, though, Cooper was still the law, so Clint drew and fired while Cooper was still confused. The bullet hit him in the right shoulder, and the gun fell from his hand to the ground. McKay grabbed the gun, stood up, and backed away.

Cooper went down on one knee, shock plain on his face.

"You didn't kill 'im," McKay said.

"I wasn't trying to," Clint said. "Where's your gun?"

"On the floor in the house."

"Okay," Clint said, "we'll have to patch him up for the ride home."

"I'll ask Mrs. Smith to give us a hand."

"Okay."

As McKay headed back to the house, Boston Corbett asked, "What the hell is goin' on?"

"It's the war, Boston," Clint said, "it's always the damn war."

# FIFTY-THREE

Mrs. Smith bandaged Cooper's wound, which, if they could get him back to town in time, would not be fatal.

"I'm not going to tie you in the saddle," Clint told Cooper, "so you better hang on. If you fall, we just might leave you."

"My job . . ." Cooper said.

"What?"

"I was just . . . doin' my job."

"No," Clint said, "you can't hide behind your job. You were about to commit murder."

Cooper opened his mouth, but he was too weak to push anything else out.

Clint walked over to where Boston Corbett was mounted. His legs had been left free so he could ride, but his hands were manacled again.

"Sorry," Clint said, "but we can't take any chances."

"I understand."

Clint walked to Eclipse and mounted up. McKay was next to him.

"Sorry about that," McKay said. "I guess I didn't know how far he'd go."

"You've got to protect me when we get back," Clint said. "I shot a lawman."

"Don't worry," McKay said. "We're the state capital, remember? You'll tell your story to the right judge."

"I hope you're right."

"If you want," McKay said, "you can go your own way. I'll take them back."

"No," Clint said, "then I'll be wondering when I'd see a poster out on me. I prefer to see it through."

"Okay," McKay said. "Let's go, then."

Arlo Huff topped a rise and saw four riders coming toward him. He backed off, dismounted, and then crawled up on the rise again, this time on his belly. He waited until they came well within range, so he could make them out. Being from town, he knew the sheriff, and he knew Lieutenant Cooper. Boston Corbett wasn't hard to pick out. That made the other man Clint Adams.

He knew he could pick one of them off from there with a rifle. But just one, and then they'd scatter. If he took out the Gunsmith, maybe the others would be easier to take along the way.

But he wasn't giving the orders. Nobody had told him to kill the Gunsmith, or either of the other two. The only one who was supposed to end up dead was Corbett.

Huff backed off the rise, mounted up again, and started riding back to the others.

"Hold up!" Ed Frame called out. "Rider comin'."

"Can you see who it is?" Dooley asked.

"Looks like Huff."

Dooley rode up alongside.

"Yeah, that's Arlo."

They waited where they were for Huff to reach them.

"They're comin'," Arlo said when he got there.

"How many?"

"Four, like you figured."

"How do they look?"

"Whataya mean?"

"I mean what kinda shape is Corbett in?" Frame asked. "You could see which one was Corbett, right?"

"I could see," Huff said. "He looked okay, but now that you mention it . . ."

"What?"

"One of the others was ridin' kinda slumped in his saddle."

"He mighta got hurt," Frame said. "That means we're lookin' at two healthy guns."

"What are we gonna do?" Lawford asked. "I mean, I don't wanna face Adams with a gun."

"We're not gonna face him," Frame said. "We're not gonna face anybody."

"Then what—"

"We'll ride back," Frame said. "That abandoned ranch we passed. There was half a barn still standing. We'll put the horses in there and spread out."

"We gonna ambush 'em?" Ben Croft asked.

"We're gonna make sure they don't know what hit 'em," Frame said.

"All four?" Huff asked. "We gonna kill all four of 'em? The law, too?"

"If we don't, we'll be lookin' at a rope," Frame said. "All of us. We'll never get to spend the money we're gonna get."

"I-I ain't never ambushed anybody before," Lawford said.

"Don't worry," Frame said. "I'll tell ya exactly what to do. Let's go."

# FIFTY-FOUR

Cooper almost fell from his saddle a couple of times, but managed to right himself in time. Clint had no intention of leaving him behind if he did fall, but it served him right to let him think so.

They were riding back the way they had come, and out of habit, Clint was looking at the ground.

"Wait a minute," he said, reining Eclipse in.

"What's wrong?" McKay asked.

"Look," Clint said, pointing to the ground.

"I thought I told you I was no tracker," McKay said. "I see tracks, yes, but what do they mean?"

"Some of them belong to us," Clint said. "See, heading in the direction we came?"

"Okay, so?"

"Then there are other tracks crossing ours."

"Somebody else could've come this way."

"But look," Clint said, "those tracks stopped, and then turned around and headed back the way they had gone. Back toward town."

"So they were tracking us?"

"Looks like it," Clint said. "They must have sent someone scouting ahead."

"And when he saw us coming, he came back and reported to the others."

"So they turned around," Clint said. "Back along the trail, they're looking for a place to ambush us."

"The old Bundy place," McKay said. "That would be perfect."

"Can we go around?"

They both looked over at Boston Corbett, who had asked the question.

"We could do that," McKay said. "There's a long way to the hospital, but I don't know if Cooper would last that long."

"What about Topeka?" Clint asked. "We could head there. Then we could take Cooper to the town doctor."

"That's even longer," McKay said. "The ride would kill him."

"We could leave him behind so he's not jostled," Clint said, "bring a doctor back to him."

"We don't even know if they're waitin' there or not," McKay said. "Let's find out before we make a decision."

"Okay," Clint said. "I'll ride ahead and find out."

"I'll go with you," McKay said. "We can leave Corbett and Cooper here."

Clint looked back at the two men. Cooper was almost unconscious. Corbett was weak, but was he too weak to attempt an escape? Now that he had a horse?

"You better stay here, McKay," Clint said. "Come on, we'll take Cooper down and lay him out somewhere."

Together they took Cooper from his horse and found a flat place to lay him down. Corbett was still mounted.

"Are you afraid Corbett will run away?" McKay asked Clint.

"Maybe he's not thinking that now," Clint said, "but if we leave him here with Cooper . . ."

"He might not be able to resist the temptation to run."

"Right."

"But if you go alone . . . how many do you think there are, from looking at the tracks?"

"Four, maybe five."

"That's too many for you to face."

"I won't face them," Clint said. "I'll just determine whether or not they're waiting for us. Then I'll come back and get you."

"We'll have to leave Corbett here alone eventually. But not with a horse. And we can leave his ankles manacled."

"That would be leaving him here unprotected," Clint said. "Look, we can deal with that later. Let me just ride ahead and see what I can find out. I'll be right back, McKay. The Bundy place can't be that far."

"All right, Adams," McKay said. "All right. But if you're not back in a couple of hours, I'm coming ahead. And I may just give Corbett a gun and bring him with me."

"You'd have to trust him, McKay," Clint said. "You'd have to really trust him."

"I know," McKay said. "And even you don't, not completely."

"I told you before," Clint said, "I know him, but not real well."

"You trusted him with that money, though," McKay reminded him. "And you turned out to be right."

"But his life hangs in the balance, this time," Clint said.

"Well then," McKay said, "I guess you just better get your ass back here."

# FIFTY-FIVE

"What if they don't come this way?" Dooley asked Ed Frame.

"Why wouldn't they?" Frame asked. "This is the way they went, this is the way they'll come to get back to the asylum."

Frame and Dooley were inside the half a barn that had been left standing after the Bundy place burned down. The horses were standing quietly with them.

The other men were scattered about the grounds, taking up positions in hiding. They had been advised that no one fired until Frame did. They had to be sure that all four men were in range and could be taken out with the first volley. Each man had been assigned one of the men to shoot at. Frame and Dooley were both going to fire at Clint Adams, since he was the most dangerous.

Frame thought his plan should work perfectly. Then they'd leave the bodies there and return to the hospital. The bodies would be found eventually, but no one would be the wiser about who had killed the men.

Or would they?

As they sat there waiting, Frame began to wonder about the other four men. The two men from town were supposed to leave with their money, but what if they didn't? What if they decided to stay because that was where they lived? And what if one of them opened his mouth?

And what about the two orderlies? They were supposed to take their money, leave their jobs, and move elsewhere. What if they didn't? And what if one of them talked to someone? Maybe a whore he was looking to impress. Frame didn't want to get sent up for murder because of somebody's pillow talk.

"What are you thinkin' so hard about?" Dooley asked.

Frame looked at him. What he was thinking was, what if more than four men were killed here today? What if he was able to kill one or two more, without the others knowing he'd done it? Maybe they'd think it happened during the gun battle. Then later, after they returned to town, and to the hospital, he could take care of the other two. And then he'd be safe.

Unless . . . unless the director decided to talk.

Frame shook his head. Now he remembered why he had given up this life and gone to work as an orderly in an asylum. At least you knew what to expect from crazy people.

"Nothin'," he said. "I ain't thinkin' about nothin'."

# FIFTY-SIX

Clint rode Eclipse hard for a period of time, but as he approached the Bundy place, he slowed down. He was able to follow the tracks, as they were very clear. He was now sure there were five men, and they were riding toward the Bundy ranch, but had they stopped there?

This was chancy. There were five men possibly lying in wait to ambush them. If even one of them spotted him, the job would be up. Then there'd be five against one and he'd be at a great disadvantage. Still, he had to get close enough to see if they had stopped there.

Who had sent the five men out? he wondered. The director? Perhaps Cooper's boss? Or could it have been the governor himself? What kind of a threat was Boston Corbett to anyone that they had to send that many men?

All the man had done was shoot John Wilkes Booth after Booth had killed Lincoln. Even though the army had tried to court-martial him, Corbett had actually just done his job. After that a man should have been allowed to live his life, Clint thought, without being reviled and hunted.

Maybe it was true.

Maybe the South *would* never die.

"You should go," Boston Corbett said, handing McKay back the canteen.

"I know I should."

Corbett looked at Cooper, who had slipped into unconsciousness.

"That man needs help," Corbett said. "So does Mr. Adams."

"I know that, okay?" McKay snapped. "I know it."

"I-I ain't gonna go nowhere," Corbett said. "I promise."

"You do, huh?"

They were seated with their backs against a boulder, chewing jerky and passing the canteen back and forth.

"Yes, I do."

"And you'll keep that promise, right?" McKay said. "The minute I'm out of sight, you won't mount up and try to get away?"

"With my feet manacled this way? How am I gonna get on a horse? How far would I get ridin' a horse like a sack of potatoes thrown over the saddle?"

McKay knew Adams was in danger. He had two choices. Leave Corbett behind or give him a gun and take him with him.

"You don't wanna give me a gun, I know that," Corbett said. "Truth is, I'm kinda weak and probably wouldn't do you much good anyway. Why don't you just go and take the horses? Then you'd know I can't get anywhere."

Trailing the horses behind him would slow him down.

He might get to the Bundy place too late, and then if Adams was dead, he'd be in deep trouble himself. He was fairly sure he and Adams could handle the five men between then, but alone? Either one would be at risk. And if the five got by Clint Adams, he and Corbett and Cooper were sitting ducks.

"Besides, Mr. Adams really doesn't need—"

"Okay, okay, shut up," McKay said.

Corbett shut up.

"I'm only gonna tell you this once," McKay said, getting to his feet. "If you run away, I'll hunt you down. I won't stop until I find you.'

"I won't run away."

"I want your word," McKay said. "The same word you gave Adams years ago when he gave you that money. You gave him your word you wouldn't run away with it."

"Actually," Corbett said, "I just told him it would be there when he came back. I never gave my word—"

"Well, I want your word now," McKay said. "I want your word on the life of the man you avenged. I want your word on the life of Abraham Lincoln."

McKay stared at Corbett, who stared back.

"I want your word as 'Lincoln's Avenger.'"

Boston Corbett made a face. "I hate that name."

"Your word."

"I wish people would stop callin' me that," Boston Corbett said.

"Your word, Corbett!"

"You got no idea what it's like to hear yourself called that all the—"

"Damn it, man! I have to go. I need your word . . . now!" McKay shouted.

"You've got it!" Corbett shouted back. "You have my word."

McKay stared at him.

"Well," Corbett said, "what the hell are you waitin' for. Go!"

# FIFTY-SEVEN

Clint approached the Bundy place on foot. There was no high vantage point he could use, so he had to approach it on level ground. That meant he had to get closer to find out what he wanted. Or he could try circling around to see if there were any tracks leaving the place. That would take a while, though. He'd have to move slowly, and quietly. If the five men were there, they'd be spread out. The chances of him running into just one of them were good. If he couldn't subdue the man quietly, it would alert the others. Then the odds would only be a slightly better four-to-one. And his other problem was he had no idea how proficient these men would be with their guns.

He had to make up his mind. There was plenty of day-light left, so darkness was not a possible ally. Move closer and take a chance on being seen, or circle around and stumble into somebody.

He decided his best bet was simply to get as close as he could, as fast as he could, and get back to where he'd left McKay and the others.

* * *

"You hear somethin'?" Dooley asked.

"Shhh," Frame said.

"I thought I heard somethin'."

"Shut up, or he'll hear you. It could've been one of our men."

"Frame, what're you gonna do with your money?" Dooley whispered.

Frame turned his head and glared at the man.

"Do I have to put a bullet in you to shut you up?" he asked.

"Okay, okay," Dooley said.

He was starting to get impatient. Frame knew if any of the others were getting impatient, they might give their position away.

He could have gotten more experienced gunnies for this job, if he'd had enough time. Then maybe he wouldn't be thinking about pulling the trigger himself on these men, just to make sure he was protected. With experienced men, at least you could trust them to keep their damned mouths shut—before, during, and after!

Clint was close enough to smell their horses. He was on his belly, behind some brush, and had moved there so quietly even he hadn't realized just how close he had come.

He could smell the horses, and he could hear somebody breathing.

It was then he realized he was practically right next to somebody whose heavy breathing would probably one day get him killed.

One of the patients in Edgewood had once asked Tom Lawford why he breathed so hard. To that point in his life

nobody had ever mentioned it to him, so he had never noticed it.

"What do you care?" had been his answer.

What the hell was the difference how hard he breathed?
The point was to keep breathing, right?

Clint wondered if that kind of deep breathing could affect a
man's hearing. He knew how the wind sounded when it
was blowing in his ear. Was that what it sounded like in this
man's ears?

He certainly would not have liked to be out in Indian
country with a man who breathed that heavily.

Well, he'd gotten this close without alerting the man; he
probably could get away, too. But he hated to lose the
chance to take one of these men out of the play. And get
some information while he was at it.

He backed out the way he had come, then moved a couple of feet to his right and came up behind the man. He
stuck the barrel of his gun into the man's back, felt him
stiffen.

"What the—" the man said.

"Shhh," Clint said. "We'll alert the others."

"What others?"

"If you're going to start out lying to me," Clint said,
"why do I need you alive?"

"Y-you wouldn't shoot me," the man stammered. "The
others would hear."

"What others?" Clint asked. "Isn't that what you asked
me?"

"You wouldn't shoot," the man said. "I could yell—"

"My friend," Clint said, "we better both hope you're not
that brave, or that stupid. If you're that brave, I'll have to

kill you first. And if you're that stupid—well, you get the idea."

"W-whataya want?"

"How many men?"

"C-countin' me?"

"Yes," Clint said, patiently, "counting you."

"F-five."

"Where?"

"Two in the barn," the man said. "I—I don't know where the other two are."

"Who's in charge?"

"A man named Frame."

"Who is he?"

"Used ta hire out as a gun, but now he works in the hospital as an orderly. He got tired of gun work."

"Then why do this?"

"The money was too good to pass up."

"And you and the other men?"

"Two orderlies, two of us from town. We got guns, but we're not professionals."

"Who's paying the freight for this little hunting trip?"

"Frame said his director was payin', but I don't know who actually put up the money."

Clint tried to think of some more questions, but he thought he had what he needed.

"Okay, friend," he said. "Thanks."

"Y-you ain't gonna kill me, are ya?"

Clint hit the man on the head with a rock—didn't want to risk damaging his gun—and said, "No."

# FIFTY-EIGHT

Clint could still smell the horses. They had to be in the barn with the two men. Now he had to work his way around behind the barn without being seen.

He hoped there were some more heavy breathers in the bunch.

Sheriff McKay came upon Clint's horse, and rightly assumed Clint had gone on from there on foot. The sheriff dismounted, tied off his horse, and set out that way himself.

"This is takin' too long." Dooley said, speaking slowly and in a whisper.

Frame would have shot him then and there if it wouldn't have made so much noise.

He ignored him.

"Frame—"

"Shut . . . up!"

That's when he saw Sheriff McKay, foolishly out in the open.

*  *  *

Clint heard a man say, "Shut . . . up!" from inside the barn. He had worked his way to the back without running into anyone else. He was a little more relaxed about the maneuver now that he knew he was dealing with amateurs.

There was only half a barn, so there were only two walls. That meant he didn't have to worry about getting a door open.

He stepped around the wall and saw two men by the front door, peering outside.

Before he could say or do anything, though, he heard a shot, and a man yell.

The sheriff moved slowly and as quietly as he could toward the Bundy place. No house and half a barn—that meant the men had to be in the barn. He started moving that way with his gun drawn.

From behind the sheriff, hidden in some bushes, Arlo Huff saw the lawman moving toward the barn. He knew Frame had said nobody fired before him, but this was too good to pass up.

He stood up, fired, and missed.

The shot went wide past the sheriff, who yelled, turned, and fired. He caught in the chest the man who had just tried to back-shoot.

Then he felt something punch him in the back of the shoulder.

Frame saw the sheriff turn and fire at Huff, hitting the man in the chest. Frame drew his gun and fired, hitting the sheriff in the back.

"You got 'im!" Dooley shouted.

"Jesus," Frame said, and shot Dooley.

Clint was shocked to see the man shoot his own man.

"Hold it!"

The man turned and stared at Clint.

"You Frame?" he asked.

"That's right."

"You should've stayed retired."

"You got that right."

Frame tried to bring his gun up, but Clint shot him.

Ben Croft came out of hiding when he saw both Huff and the sheriff go down.

"What's goin' on!" he shouted.

The sheriff shot him from the ground.

Tom Lawford, who had come to, staggered out into the open, one hand on his head, the other holding his gun. He started pulling the trigger, dizzily firing into the ground.

McKay shot him, too.

Clint came out of the barn and rushed to where McKay lay on his stomach. He could see that the man had taken a bullet to the left shoulder.

"McKay." He grabbed him and turned him over.

"We get 'em all?" McKay gasped.

"We got 'em."

"I stumbled into the play like an amateur. Thought they'd all be in the barn."

"It's okay. It's over."

"How bad am I?"

"Not too bad. I'll patch you up, and as long as we get you to a doctor, you'll be fine."

"You find out who sent 'em?"

Clint nodded.

"Director Desmond. He'll have a lot of explaining to do when we get back. Maybe he'll turn in whoever gave him the order."

"The governor? Fat chance."

"We'll see."

"I left . . . Corbett with . . . Cooper. Guess that'll . . . turn out to be a . . . a mistake, too.

"No, it won't."

"You think he'll be there when we get back?"

Clint nodded.

"He'll be there."

# HISTORICAL NOTE

After Boston Corbett escaped from the asylum near Topeka—it was *not* called Edgewood—it was said he went to Mexico and was never heard from again.